Billy Huddle
and the Mirror of
Enchantment

Misti June,

The Power is in You!!!

Zach

Misti

Printed in the United States of America.

First Printing: June 2011

ISBN-978-0-9836542-0-9

This book is dedicated to the ones who give me a reason for taking a breath each and every day. Life has been an adventure, but with the loving support of my gorgeous wife and wonderful children, I have been able to pour my imagination into this book. In my family, I have found my own power. For that, I am truly thankful.

Contents

One

Just another school day / 9

Two

Lions and tigers and mo-mos, oh my! / 19

Three

Daily chores / 33

Four

A funny thing happened on the way to the ship / 46

Five

Flying and falling / 59

Six

Welcome to the temple / 73

Seven

The breakfast buffet / 85

Eight

Time to quit / 100

Nine
Smile for the birdie / 114

Ten
Have wings, can travel / 129

Eleven
Home is where the wizard is / 142

Twelve
Imps on the run / 155

Thirteen
It takes one to know one / 168

Fourteen
Things aren't what they used to be / 182

Fifteen
Help from an old friend / 195

Sixteen
The power of friendship / 210

Billy Huddle and the Mirror of Enchantment

By Zach Chandler

Chapter One
Just another school day

$\mathfrak{J}$ust by looking at this creepy, aged house, you could never understand why a thirteen-year-old boy would dare to go into it, let alone want to. The house was run down and surrounded by an iron gate that was more rust than iron. Inside the gate, the grass had grown as tall as Billy was, and the large wooden front porch would creak and crack as you walked across it.

Billy didn't bother knocking anymore because inside was the only person who really paid attention to him or even seemed to want him around, Old Man Richardson.

Old Man Richardson was a frail elderly man who never smiled at anyone, including Billy. His back was crooked and he walked with a cane that had a dull black stone in the handle. He had lost most of his hair, and what little he did have was grey and thin. His skin was wrinkled and he wasn't very clean, but he gave Billy one thing he never received from anyone else: attention.

Sitting at his kitchen table, the old man would wait for Billy with a warm drink that tasted something like sweet apple cider and honey. As he handed the drink to Billy every day, he would say the same thing: "I put my heart and soul into that drink for you, my boy."

Every now and then, Billy even thought he saw Old Man Richardson smile. He would wait in complete silence except for his quiet breathing until Billy had finished every drop of the delicious drink— and then he would tell Billy the most wonderful stories.

In all the stories he heard Old Man Richardson tell, Billy most enjoyed hearing about the Flow. The Flow was the magical force that Old Man Richardson said was special to every creature. It was what made the ixion run so fast and allowed the shadow creatures to never be seen.

"The Flow," he had said, "was in everything, and it was the responsibility of those who knew it existed to harness and use it. By controlling this force, a person would have great power and there would be no limit to what he could do."

Billy listened to the elderly man talk until well after dark, hanging on his every word. He felt like he was doing more than just listening to an old man's stories; he was learning about the world around him as he hoped it would be. Before he left to go home, he asked Mr. Richardson why he took the time to share the stories with him day after day. After all, hardly anyone else even spoke to him, and when they did the words were definitely not kind.

The old man just stared back at him with the same stone-faced stare and said, "Because I see room inside of you for them… and there is power in you, too."

Walking home, Billy thought about what was spoken by the old man.

There is power in me?

How in the world could power be in me?

He was glad that Old Man Richardson had not seen the millions of spit wads flying at his head, or the jr. high giant Oscar picking on him time and time again. He was happy his friend had not seen him hiding under the bleachers during recess every day because he couldn't keep up with the stronger kids, and thankful his friend never saw him daydreaming about a dried-up piece of gum on the back of a school bus seat. If his elderly friend could see who he really was, power was definitely not what he would see.

Arriving home, he quietly slipped through the living room and up the stairs to his room. Climbing into his bed, he gazed out of his window to the stars. Watching them twinkle in the sky, he thought of all the amazing stories he had been told. He wondered which one of those stars was near that magical place he wanted to be. Drifting to sleep, he heard the words of the old man once again, "The power is in you."

The next morning his usual seat on the bus felt just like it always did, with that annoying spring pushing up out of it. Billy thought that he would be used to it by now, but as he sat there riding along on old bus number fourteen, it was just as uncomfortable as it always had been.

Taking this bumpy ride to school with him was the same 43 children, doing their best to ignore him and the same sticky piece of gum on the seat, he had seen eighty-four days in a row. The gum was something to focus on besides the other students on the bus. Sometimes it would magically transform before his eyes as he stared at it, as if it were a cloud. Hideous monsters, magical puffs of smoke, and towering statues are just a few things the hardened piece of gum became. It took his mind from the babbling of other school children on their way to Ratcliff Jr. High School. Then, like always, the bus would pull up to the school and he would get out—but the daydreaming would not stop.

It's not that he didn't like school, or that he didn't want to learn. It was just hard for him to find much interest in the world around him when the world taking place in his imagination was so much more fun and exciting. Other kids would go out of their way to make fun of him and tease him relentlessly.

Sure, he never had designer clothes or the newest style of shoes, but it wasn't his fault his parents hardly knew he existed, much less care what he wore. Of course, his short brown hair was a bit messy, but no more than that of any other young boy becoming a teenager.

Today was pretty much like any other day. He started out in homeroom and, after taking notes and having a spit wad or twenty thrown at the back of his head, headed off to his second class. The next period was basically a repeat of the first, except that Oscar was in this class.

Billy could never really understand what he did to make Oscar dislike him, but Oscar always had time to stick his spit-covered finger in Billy's ear. Any of the kids would have told you that Oscar was a jr. high giant. Rumor was he was really supposed to have graduated from high school by now, but enjoyed torturing people smaller than him so much that he kept failing on purpose.

Lunch time would arrive with a crazy madness that only a Jr. High lunch period could provide. Lunch trays crashing, children chattering, and a monitor saying, "You better be quiet, or we will eat lunch silently" a thousand times were common occurrences in this swirling circus of a room.

Billy had his place too, at a table by himself in the corner, and he loved it. While some people may have been saddened by eating in a lunch room by themselves, Billy looked forward to this part of the day. He would watch the children scurry about and imagine that they were the ant people of Talamary Forest gathering food for their home. Seeing Henry Waltham eat eight slices of pizza, he couldn't help but wonder if he could hold his own with one of the Crumber Creatures. Billy's imagination raced to the stories he had heard so many times when he looked at, listened to, and even smelled the chaos of that room.

The lunch bell would ring at the end of the period and drag him back to reality, at least long enough to get through his next few classes. His afternoon seemed to take ages as he sat, trying to be busy and focus on his work. But he was really just counting the minutes until the last bell rang. Then, climbing back onto old Bus Number Fourteen, he would daydream away, staring at that same dry piece of gum once more.

The bus ride home filled him with excitement. When he finally got home every day, he would get to see the only person Billy ever really considered to call his friend and spend a few hours caught in the world he dreamed was his reality.

He didn't even bother going into his house after climbing out of the school bus. After all, both his parents worked until almost nine every night and no one would know if he had come or gone. Instead, he raced down the block as quickly as he could to the two-story house on the corner.

Making it to the old rundown house, he walked into the kitchen ready to drink his delicious drink and hear more of the stories he had waited to hear. Today, however, was different. There was no warm drink, no familiar breathing, and no old man to tell him stories. For the first time in a long time, Billy did not feel it was okay to be alone.

He sat at the table silently for hours. He just knew that any minute the old man would arrive and begin to fill his cup with sweet apple cider and his head with stories like those that he had in the past. *How could he be late, and what could have happened to him?*

For two years, he had always come over to the house, and not once had his friend not been there. He walked home slowly in complete silence.

Arriving home, he found his parents in the kitchen. As he was adopted, he had never had a warm relationship with either of them, and in truth he kind of liked it that way.

His dad looked up as Billy came in the door. "I guess you heard there were cops and an ambulance down at that old geezer Richardson's house earlier today?"

Billy's lip began to tremble. "What?"

"Rumor is that he didn't make it," said his mom. "I'm kind of glad too. That guy seemed to be making you weirder by the day."

Billy climbed into his bed with his eyes filled with tears. *Could my only friend, the only one who cared anything about me, really be gone?* he thought.

Billy fell asleep sobbing. Tonight, for the first night since he could remember, no stars seemed to shine.

After lunch the next day, Oscar saw Billy in the hall. "Hey freak boy! Did you hear about that crazy old man you like to hang out with? I heard that dirty creep finally died, and good riddance too. He was a nasty freak just like you!"

Billy felt his skin go white-hot with anger. Hearing those words, he almost felt that attacking Oscar could somehow bring his friend back, so he jumped on him, swinging punches wildly. When others stepped in to break up the fight, he found himself alone again, sitting and waiting outside the principal's office.

Sitting there with his head in his hands and a throbbing pain behind his eyes, he thought *this can't be real. The old man... my friend... is gone?*

He wouldn't be hearing any more stories. There would be no more warm drinks or tales of magic. He was really all alone.

At that moment, with all his emotions churning inside of him, he got up, ran out the door, and didn't stop running. Tears filled his eyes as he made his way past the park and old Settler's Pond. The sky filled with clouds, and rain began to fall. Slowly, the light rain became steadier and more intense until he was running in a downpour.

As he arrived at the old man's house drenched by the rain, lightning flickered across the sky. He walked across the creaking front porch and through the doorway. Even though the thunder made incredible crashes of noise, and the rain pelted the roof, to Billy there was nothing but silence.

This can't be my life, he thought.

This can't be the way it's supposed to be.

At that moment, Billy heard a thud from upstairs. He had never walked up the staircase, nor had he seen the old man go up or come down it.

Only the sound of the falling rain filled his head as he stood there, puzzled and shivering. Then, the loud thud sounded again, causing his heart to skip a beat. He walked tentatively up the steps of the old staircase as the boards creaked beneath his feet.

Coming to the top of the staircase, he saw a short hallway before him. The paint was peeling and there was an old musty smell in the air. It was not very inviting at all, but the thought of finding his friend moved him forward. He heard the loud thud a third time, and could tell for certain now that it was coming from the last door on the end.

He cautiously put one foot in front of the other and walked to the door. Holding his breath, he turned the dull brass knob and slowly pushed the door open. The door made an eerie creak, and Billy felt a cold draft blow against his face as he walked into the room.

This part of the house seemed untouched by the years, and the walls were completely bare. Though the area was a bit dirty, a fresh fragrance filled the room. No furniture could be found, except for a tall object in the center of the room covered by a dusty old sheet. He pulled the sheet gently, and it softly fell to the floor, revealing a full-size mirror with a dark brown wooden frame.

Symbols unlike any Billy had ever seen before were carved into the wood. *It must be another language* he thought as he gazed at the symbols etched into the finely crafted wood. As he reached out to touch one of the symbols, he noticed something happening to the mirror itself.

No longer did he see his reflection, but running water flowing across what would normally be glass. It made no sound as it moved effortlessly down in a crystal blue sheet. Billy reached out to touch it with his finger.

At that moment, everything went dark.

Chapter Two
Lions and tigers and mo-mos, oh my!

Blinking a couple of times, Billy's eyes slowly adjusted to the light of the room.

Where am I?

A young boy about his age startled him. His hair was messy and his clothes a bit ragged, but there he stood, staring back at him with large blue eyes.

"My name is Joey. You have been asleep for a long time," he said with a puzzled look on his face.

"Billy... Billy's my name... Where am I?"

"Turnshire, of course," Joey replied as the door swung open.

A person Billy thought was Joey's mother stomped noisily into the room. She had long brown hair, but the same deep blue eyes.

"And how are we feeling today, young man?" the woman asked briskly. "You must have hit your head very hard indeed. You have been out for two whole days."

"Yeah," added Joey, "My dad pulled you out of the river at the bottom of Glacier Falls. Wasn't very smart being in them waters at this time of year. What were you thinking?"

"Joey! Mind your manners and don't ask so many questions," the woman said. "And pour our guest a glass of water. Now where are you from, my boy?"

Billy started to reply, but then saw something so amazing he couldn't get the words out of his mouth. On the little table by the wall, across from his bed, a pitcher slowly elevated and began pouring water into a glass.

No one had even touched it. It simply did it on its own.

In disbelief, he looked around to see if anyone else was seeing this, or if he really was going crazy. That's when he noticed Joey, with his arm outstretched in the direction of the pitcher. In his hand, he held something Billy had only heard about in stories.

"Is that a wand?" asked Billy as he stared with his eyes wide at the sight of the gnarled wooden stick in Joey's hand.

"Of course it is," he replied, "and I'm getting much better, I think."

Joey spoke as if using the wand was no big deal, as if using it was just another task as simple as tying his shoelaces. With a small flick of the wrist, Joey sent the glass of water smoothly floating over to him.

"Thank you," Billy said as he took a drink of the cool water.

"My name is Mrs. McGregor," said the woman, looking down from behind small round glasses. "Whereabouts are you from? Hillsbury... Thumbledrop?"

"No ma'am. I'm from Hartford, in Connecticut," Billy quietly said.

"Well now, I've never heard of that place before," said Mrs. McGregor. "Best we let you get some rest, and we can talk about it when you get your wits about you."

At that, Mrs. McGregor dimmed the little lamp in the room and tucked the sheets up around him. She and Joey quietly left the room leaving him to rest.

Billy thought that Mrs. McGregor was such a nice woman, although a bit loud. You would think being in a strange place would have made Billy uneasy, but he slept as peacefully as he had slept in days, if not years.

As Billy awoke the next morning, the sun peeked through the curtains of the small window in the room. He felt much better than he had the evening before.

Slowly climbing out of bed and standing up, he heard the sounds of pots and pans from the other room and smelled the most delicious aromas.

"Come on in, my boy," he heard from beyond the bedroom door.

Billy straightened his shirt and walked into a large, brightly lit room. It was spacious and encompassed the living and dining area as well as the kitchen.

"You come on in and have a seat while Joey sets the table," said Mrs. McGregor. "You could use a good meal."

Billy watched as Joey began gently setting the dishes on the table with flicks of his wrist and waves of his wand. Billy had only dreamed of such amazing things. *How could they be possible?*

Suddenly, the front door of the house swung open and a rather large man with a coarse brown beard and thick glasses walked in. He smiled lovingly at Mrs. McGregor as he entered the room.

"Hello, my dear," he said as he gave her a hug. "How are we today?"

"Better than Beetle Bread," she replied, giggling.

"Looks like our sleeping stranger has finally awakened," said the large man with a deep raspy voice. "I'm Mr. McGregor."

"Billy, sir... Billy Huddle."

"Well I am most pleased to meet you, young Billy," said Mr. McGregor as he reached out and shook Billy's hand. His hands were large and dry, and his handshake was strong. "How is it you came to be in the river lad?"

"I don't really know, sir."

Billy went on to tell the family all he could remember. He told them about the old man and the house, about the rain and the mirror. The McGregor family listened intently as Mrs. McGregor piled savory meats, cheeses, and breads onto their plates for the morning's breakfast. After Billy finished telling them all he could remember, he noticed the family staring back at him in a quite peculiar way.

"Well now," said Mr. McGregor, "it appears you hit your head a bit harder than expected, quite hard indeed. You are welcome to stay with us until you get your wits about you and we figure out where you belong."

"Thank you, sir," said Billy.

"Now dig in," said Mrs. McGregor, setting the last heaping portions of food on the table.

Billy and the rest of the family ate until they were well beyond full. The meal was as good a meal as Billy had ever eaten. After everyone was finished, Mrs. McGregor gathered the plates and began washing them in the sink.

"Why are you doing that by hand, Mom?" asked Joey, reaching for his wand that he kept handily at his belt. "I can get them done faster for you if you want."

"Because some people still understand the value of hard work, and it would do you good to remember it too every now and again," said Mrs. McGregor with a scolding look on her face.

Joey quickly put his wand back to his side.

"Why don't you take our new house guest down to the river and see if it will help him remember anything," she said, motioning toward the door.

The two boys made their way out the front door, and Billy got his first glimpse of Turnshire. It was a rather small community, with little shops located on one main street. The wood-framed buildings were very aged, but well kept by their owners. Signs like *Mr. Standish's Grocer and Components Shop*, and *Patterson's Perfect Powders* could be seen above the buildings.

"We can stop by and pick up some supplies for mom on the way back." Joey said with a smirk on his face. "Maybe surprise her since heading down to the river is getting me out of most of my chores."

Joey led Billy to a little trail on the outskirts of town. It was heavily overgrown, and appeared to become more overgrown as it proceeded further into the forest.

There was an old weathered sign posted on a tree at the beginning of the trail:

PROCEED WITH CAUTION
MOMORDI IN SEASON

"What's a momordi?" Billy asked, quite startled by the sign, "And why do we need to proceed with caution?"

"You don't have to worry about those mo-mos, as we like to call them," said Joey. "Those little boogers won't even know we are walking through, as long as we keep quiet."

Billy followed Joey in almost complete silence. In fact, he did not say a word and even took special care to step exactly where Joey stepped. Walking down the winding path, it didn't seem nearly as dark as he had imagined. It was damp, and often there were logs or fallen branches to step over or go around, but the longer they walked, the more relaxed he became.

Billy marveled at the different colors that he saw as he and his new friend made their way down the trail. Oranges, reds, blues, and every color of flower lined the forest floor and clung to the trunks of many trees. Birds sang and other animals unlike any he had ever heard chattered quietly in the tree tops. It was almost as if the creatures of this forest were talking to one another. Though he had never been in the forest before, it became more and more familiar with every step, almost welcoming him.

Just when Billy had become quite comfortable with the many noises of the forest, it grew alarmingly silent. Joey stopped moving and stood completely still on the path ahead of him.

"Uh oh," Joey whispered.

"Uh oh.... What's uh oh?" Billy replied with a somewhat frantic breath.

Joey put his hand up to his ear. "Uh oh means to follow me... now!"

Joey took off running through the forest away from the path they had been walking. Billy raced after him, his beautiful, magnificent forest suddenly quite scary. He no longer heard pleasant noises from birds and animals in the trees. All he heard was a grumbling and gurgling that followed them as it rustled across the forest floor in pursuit.

"Just keep running!" said Joey. "We have to make it to the old monkey puzzle tree."

Billy followed just as fast as his legs would carry him. He had no idea what was making those strange noises, but he was quite sure he didn't want to find out, and they were getting louder.

Joey and Billy burst into a small clearing just when Billy felt he could run no further. With Billy close on Joey's heels, they sprinted to a giant tree in the middle of the clearing and quickly scurried up it. Once Billy was securely sitting next to Joey on an intricately braided together tree branch, gasping for breath, he looked down from his position well up the tree at the dreaded mo-mos circling beneath them.

The mo-mos were frog-like creatures, about the size of a small dog. They didn't hop around, but rather walked, a bit clumsily, as they smelled around the base of the tree. A thick slime dripped from two rows of sharp teeth that were easily seen when they opened their mouths. They grumbled and growled to one another in what seemed to be some form of communication.

"So what are we supposed to do now?" Billy asked with a nervous quiver in his voice. "They can't climb trees, can they?"

"Nah, they're not much for climbing trees. We just have to wait a bit until they move on," laughed Joey, very amused by how scared Billy was.

"Isn't there anything you can do? You know, with your wand?" Billy's eyes bulged at the sight of the hideous creatures.

"I only know the easy stuff right now," Joey replied. "I don't head off to formal training for another couple of months. Then, I hope to become a mage as powerful as any have ever been."

"A mage?" Billy asked.

"You know, a mage... a wizard," said Joey. "This isn't a perfect world, everybody knows that. If it was, we wouldn't be stuck up a tree."

Joey laughed, looking down at the mo-mos still pacing the ground. "The mages are the chosen few that help maintain order in our world. They make sure that the bad things don't get too strong and that everything is kept in balance."

Billy listened, hanging on every word Joey said. "So how do the mages maintain order if there are so many bad things in the world?"

Joey held his wand up to the light. "That is what a mage does, and what I am going to become. A high mage is trained to be a powerful wizard, and with their abilities they watch over the world and maintain that balance between good and evil."

Billy looked down the tree at the creatures circling below them. "Evil...?"

"Evil, dark, bad, you name it," Joey said. "It's a mage's responsibility to keep them all in check. Right now, we need to be quiet though, or those evil, dark, bad little guys aren't going anywhere." The boys both laughed quietly and then began waiting in silence for the mo-mos to move on.

As Billy and Joey waited among the intricate branches of the tree for a while, the aggressive little creatures grew tired of simply sniffing around the base and walked back into the woods. After climbing down the tree, Billy and Joey started walking (more cautiously than before) to the river.

Before long, Billy began to hear the sound of the running water, and it got louder with each step. Walking out of the woods, he could see they had arrived at a huge waterfall that appeared to continue up into the clouds.

"We found you over there," Joey said, pointing to a beach-like area with little crab creatures scurrying across it. "Does any of this look familiar?"

Looking across the sandy bank and then up at the waterfall, his mind immediately recalled the water he had seen flowing in place of the mirror in that upstairs room. He thought about the symbols on the dark wooden frame, and how the moment he touched them the glass began to flow. Billy picked up a stick and drew the symbol he remembered in the sand.

"Know what this means," he asked, pointing the stick at the symbol. Joey immediately kicked sand over it and erased it with his foot.

"We're not supposed to make that mark," he said, appearing as startled as Billy had been by the mo-mos.

"But do you know what it means?" Billy asked.

"It means the dark one…. That's his mark, and we are not supposed to make it," Joey said, shaking his head. "When he was around, there was not much good to be found, they say."

With that, he turned around and started walking back down the trail. The hike to town was a quiet one. Joey was tense, and it was obvious that it wasn't about the possibility of the mo-mos coming back.

What could have happened, Billy wondered. *And who is the dark one?*

He figured now was not the time to ask any more questions, so he just quietly followed Joey back.

Arriving back at town, the sun was already low in the sky. The two boys headed to Mr. Standish's Shop to pick up the supplies for Mrs. McGregor. Walking into the store, Billy realized this was not like any grocery store he had ever been in before. Sure, there were your everyday garden essentials. Leafy greens, fruits, and vegetables of every type were well represented, but another section was labeled magical medicines and herbs. This section brimmed with things with very odd names such as mugwort, orris root, and rowan berry.

Standing proudly behind the counter of the store was none other than Mr. Standish himself. He was a short, dumpy sort of fellow who had very little hair. The only hair he did have in fact, was just above his ears; the top of his head was completely bald. He wore a grey suit with a bright green bowtie and had shoes so shiny you could see your reflection in them.

"What can I do for you today, boys?" he asked with a twinkle in his eyes. "I just got in a fresh supply of cordyceps that are very nice indeed."

"No thanks, Mr. Standish," said Joey. "I just need to pick up my mom's grocery order and wanted to know if you maybe had a wishy washer?"

"A wishy washer?" said Mr. Standish. "I believe I just might have one left." Mr. Standish went into the back of the store and started gathering the supplies.

"Hey Joey… what's a wishy washer?" Billy asked.

"It's kind of a fish-like creature that you keep in your dish water. Cleans up the dishes really nice," he said with a sly smile. "They also break quite a few less dishes than I do practicing my magic."

Mr. Standish returned with the supplies and the wishy washer and placed them on the counter. "Will there be anything else?" he asked.

"No, that's all Mr. Standish," Joey said as he pulled a couple of coins out of his pocket and tossed them on the counter.

"Thanks boys," said Mr. Standish. "I put a couple of pieces of locust nectar candy in there for you, too. Take care."

As they left the store, Joey had already removed his candy and popped it into his mouth. He handed the other piece to Billy.

"I guess this means you may be with us for a while," he said. "This may be fun."

"I think you may be right," said Billy, "I really think it may be."

Chapter Three
Daily chores

Shortly after Billy awoke the next day, he walked into the dining area of the McGregors' home. There, he noticed a package wrapped neatly and placed in the chair he was about to sit in.

"I hear you may be staying with us for a while," said Mrs. McGregor. "I think you may need these."

Billy opened the package to reveal a set of clothes very much like those Joey had been wearing. A brown pair of pants made from a coarse fabric, a neatly pressed shirt, and a pair of soft leather shoes all displayed Mrs. McGregor's amazing handy work.

"If you're going to stay with us for a while, you might as well fit in," Mr. McGregor said with a chuckle.

Billy picked up the pressed shirt and admired it. "Thank you... thank you very much."

Mr. McGregor smiled. "I figure you could help Joey prepare for his training at the temple, and I hear Mr. Patterson could use some help gathering herbs for his shop."

"We'll start looking right after morning chores and training," Joey said eagerly.

After another delicious breakfast, Billy went and changed into his new clothes. They were a little baggy, but very comfortable, and he enjoyed knowing he now fit in a little more.

Billy thought back, about where it was that he came from and how differently he was treated by the McGregors. Unlike his own parents, they only said kind words to him, and made him almost feel like he belonged. He would gladly deal with a hundred mo-mos if it meant he never saw a spit wad or a Jr. High giant named Oscar ever again.

"My now Billy, don't you look spiffy," said Mrs. McGregor, standing in front of the sink and admiring how efficiently her new wishy washer was cleaning the dishes, "very spiffy indeed."

"C'mon," said Joey as he pulled Billy outside to the yard. "Let's get to work."

"So what kind of chores do we have to do?" Billy asked.

"Chores and training go hand in hand if we do 'em right." said Joey. "So let's do 'em right."

Joey walked over to a large pile of logs where a heavy ax with a long wooden handle leaned. He pulled his wand from his side and stretched it out towards the ax. "*Fluxi Volatucus*," he said, and the ax slowly rose from the ground. "Now, if you'll put the logs on the big stump, I will chop 'em in half."

Splitting logs isn't usually considered an enjoyable chore in the least, but with a little magic added it was quite fun. Again and again, Billy placed a log onto the stump, and with a flick of his wrist Joey used the floating ax to chop it in two. Before long, Billy noticed Joey was becoming tired. He was breathing heavily and couldn't stop sweating.

"Are you alright?" Billy asked, quite concerned.

Joey, using his wand, slowly lowered the ax back to the ground. "Yeah... but maybe we should take a break. I'm running pretty low."

Billy and Joey sat down on the stump. All around them, split logs were scattered across the yard. Billy stared at the wood, amazed at how much work had been done in such a short time.

He picked up one of the split logs. "What did you mean when you said you were running pretty low?" Billy asked.

"On Flow," Joey said, recalling for Billy the stories of Old Man Richardson. "Those that can do magic do it because they use a special energy inside of them. When it gets all used up, you have to rest for a while for your body to make more."

"You mean the magic doesn't come from your wand?" Billy asked.

Joey chuckled and shook his head. "The magic comes from inside you, your energy. Everybody has it, but only some people can get it out. The wand just helps focus it from your body to be used."

Billy tossed the chopped log back onto the ground. "It's really amazing, that's for sure. I wish I could do it."

Joey stood up and started walking away. "Let's go. There is something I want to show you."

Billy followed Joey back off into the woods. This time, much to Billy's relief, they didn't take the path warning about the vicious little mo-mos. In fact, they took no marked path at all.

Walking along, Joey and Billy could feel the energy in the air. A soft breeze blew through the trees, and the air smelled sweet with flowers. Joey skipped ahead, hopping off branches and rocks and whistling a happy little tune.

Suddenly, a strange creature ran between the two boys on the trail. Billy froze on the spot, staring at the creature. It looked a lot like the grey squirrels that he had seen in the playground at his school, but had a bright red feathery tail and long floppy ears of the same color.

"That's just a flame tail," laughed Joey. "They are completely harmless."

The creature, apparently just as startled as Billy, quickly scampered up the nearest tree. It stopped on a branch well out of reach and turned to chatter angrily at the boys. Laughing at the small creature's annoyance, they continued walking.

The forest began to change as the two boys walked steadily uphill through the woods. The grasses, plants, and trees became increasingly vibrant. The air felt almost electric as Joey and Billy arrived at the edge of a great lake. Birds swam on the surface of the water, diving every so often for fish, and the ripples of the water reflected silvery light.

"This is it." Joey smiled as he looked across the lake. "This is how magic works."

The wind, much stronger here, came off the water's edge and blew into the boys' faces. Billy's eyes followed Joey's, to a spot across the lake. "You mean, the magic comes from the water?"

"The lake does what every lake does," said Joey. "It holds the water. Here it sits with only the power of the winds rippling it's surface"

Joey reached down and splashed the water through his fingers.

"Running off of this lake, a river goes on for miles," he said. "Sometimes the river bubbles along gently and sometimes it's a roaring rapid. Eventually, it pushes out to form the awesome power of Glacier Falls."

"You mean this lake turns into where we were yesterday?" asked Billy.

"This is exactly how magic works," Joey said. "The lake is like the magic that is in us. It sits there and waits. Sometimes it gets hot and we lose a little. Sometimes it is refreshed by rain, and replenished. It is always there though, just waiting, powerful inside us."

Billy's eyes widened as it began to make sense to him. "The river is like the wand," Joey said. "It channels the water down a path, but the power still comes from the lake pushing behind it. Eventually, once it is focused enough and the magic is pushed out quickly enough, it will flow out like the water does at Glacier Falls."

Joey took his wand and pointed it at the water. Slowly, drop after drop, water rose from the lake and formed a ball that hovered above the surface.

"So I have the power to do this inside of me?" Billy asked curiously.

"Everyone does," Joey laughed, handing his wand over to Billy. "Go on… give it a try."

Billy stretched the wand out towards the water. He felt something stirring up inside him and his muscles grew tense. He stared intensely at the water's surface, but nothing happened.

"Oh well," said Joey. "Very few people can channel the flow of magic out of them, and nobody does it on the first try."

Billy handed the wand back over to Joey, a bit disappointed.

"Let's gather some of this muckroot," said Joey as he pulled a little green plant from the ground. "It grows all around here, and I'm sure Mr. Patterson will want it."

The boys searched the area for the root. Pulling the plants was difficult, as they had grown firm and secure in the fertile ground. The lake area was much more peaceful than the mo-mo infested woods of the day before. Billy ventured around the lake's edge, confidently searching for the herb. After a bit of searching, he found a rather large hole extending into the ground.

"Hey Joey, do you know where this hole leads?" he asked, leaning forward to peer down.

"Sometimes heavy rains will open up little caverns around here. Just be careful because they aren't very stable."

No sooner had Joey given Billy the warning than the ground beneath Billy's feet slipped and crumbled away. Billy let out a startled yell, but it was too late as he tumbled head first into the hole. He slid across the wet soil and loose rocks before falling several feet down into an open cavern. Splashing into the water, he struck his left arm against a large rock. Lying in a shallow pool, soaked in the cold murky water, he looked up at the opening he had tumbled through. The trickling sunlight filtered into the cavern as his arm throbbed in pain.

Joey raced over to the edge of the hole and yelled down into the cavern. "Billy... Billy... are you alright?"

Billy wiped the water out of his eyes. "I think my arm is broken," he said, trying to move it. "I fell down a long way."

He stood up and looked around. It was grey and dark, filled with rocks and boulders from the shifting grounds. His eyes slowly began to adjust to the limited amount of light. Gazing into the darkness, he caught the reflection of two eyes staring back at him. As he held his breath he could hear his own heart beat as his eyes began to focus.

"There's some creature down here," Billy said, "and it's looking at me."

Joey tried to look down into the hole but couldn't get too close without falling in as well. "What does it look like?"

As Billy began to make out the creature, he described it to Joey. "It's about the size of a small pony, but it's covered in scales. It looks like it's trapped under a large fallen rock," Billy called up. "I think... I think it's a little dragon."

"A dragon...how many legs does it have?"

"It's got two front legs and a long snake-like tail with spikes on it," answered Billy.

"That's not a dragon you're looking at. That's a wyvern! Stay away from it," Joey said. "Those creatures are bad news!"

Looking at the animal, Billy could now clearly see a boulder pinning the creature to the cavern floor. It must have been trapped for a while, as it was making no attempt to escape. The beast peered back at Billy, and even though the creature itself was quite scary, its eyes looked gentle and soft.

"I'm throwing down a long stick that should be sharp enough to kill it," said Joey. "Just push it into the soft spot just underneath his chin, but be careful."

Joey tossed the long, sharp stick down into the hole. Picking it up, Billy stood in front of the creature with the spear raised above his head.

The wyvern gazed at Billy and raised its head, exposing its chest. Its eyes were bright green like emeralds, and seemed to look not just at Billy, but *into* him. Gripping the spear tightly with his one good arm, Billy thrust it towards the creature and deep into the soil, just under the large rock restraining the beast.

He knew it may be a huge mistake, but he couldn't kill a creature laying there defenseless. Using the long stick as a lever, he lifted the large rock off of the wyvern's body. The wyvern made a deep hissing sound, shook its head, and then jumped onto him, knocking him to his back.

The wyvern planted its feet firmly on Billy's chest and flicked its tongue into the air. Billy could hardly breathe under the weight of the creature. Then, the wyvern let out a screeching hiss and treated Billy to a dollop of warm, foul breath.

Billy knew that at any moment, he would feel the sharp bite of the wyvern. Yet, for no knowable reason, the wyvern flapped its leathery wings and flew from the cavern's entrance.

Joey yelled down into the hole. "Are you okay... Billy... Billy, are you okay?"

It took Billy a while to catch his breath. His blood was still cold with fear, and he was shaking from what had just happened. He called up to Joey. "I think I'm okay... other than my arm."

Joey lowered a long leafy vine down into the cavern and Billy tied it around his waist. Slowly, Joey pulled him out of the cavern.

"What happened?" Joey asked. "How did the wyvern escape?"

"I let him go. When I looked into his green eyes, I just couldn't kill him."

"Wyverns only have black eyes," said Joey, "Black like death, and you're lucky to be alive. Now let's go get your arm fixed up."

Billy followed Joey back through the woods, holding his injured arm close at his side. The sun was hot and the sweet fragrance of the flowers seemed to have gone away. Billy couldn't get sight of the wyvern's eyes out of his head, or stop wondering why it had not attacked him. He was certain there was some kind of connection with the animal that he couldn't explain. Maybe the creature was just scared, or simply trying to get away, but he would never know.

When they arrived back at the town, Joey pointed to an old cottage up on a hill. "That's where Mrs. Templeton lives. Some folks say she is crazy, and she would probably agree, but she's the best healer in a hundred miles."

Billy felt the intense throbbing in his arm. "Is she a doctor?"

"No, but she has healing magic down pretty well," Joey said tapping his wand. "She should be able to fix your arm up in no time."

The two boys walked up the hill and knocked on the door of the run down cottage. An elderly woman with silver hair came to the door.

"Hello… who's there now?" she said, staring straight out the doorway.

"It's me, Joey McGregor," Joey said as the woman looked down at the boys. "My friend is hurt, and I was wondering if you would help him."

The old woman slowly walked back into her home, feeling her way about and gazing straight ahead. "Well now child," said Mrs. Templeton, "sit down here and let's see what this old blind woman can make of you."

Billy walked over and sat down in the chair next to her. The aged woman reached out to Billy and began to mumble some words he couldn't understand. As she did, a very faint blue glow came off of her hand and moved slowly over his arm.

Her eyebrows raised and she nodded her head. "A broken arm, it appears. If you will get my wand, I will fix you right up. You know where it is, don't you Joey?"

Joey walked over to a cabinet and opened it. There on the shelf was a white wooden wand. It was twisted from one end to the other and had some symbols carved into it that Billy didn't understand.

The old woman took the wand, and pointing it at his arm said, "*Curatio Medicor.*"

The same blue light he had seen come from Mrs. Templeton's hand glowed much more brilliantly as it extended out of the end of her wand. She moved the wand slowly back and forth across the broken arm and gradually the dull pain went away.

"There now, that should feel a bit better," she said.

Billy moved his arm. The pain had completely gone away, and he moved it easily once again.

He flexed his fingers and extended his arm, amazed at the way it now felt. "Thank you… thank you, ma'am…"

"'Tis nothing at all," said the old woman. "You boys need to take better care of yourselves though."

The boys thanked Mrs. Templeton again and started walking home. "So what are we going to do now?" said Billy.

"There's always a lot to do in this little town," said Joey as he laughed, "but first we got to explain to dad why the chores aren't done."

Chapter Four

A funny thing happened on the way to the ship

There were so many interesting people and amazing things to see around the little community of Turnshire. Now, as Billy was prepared to see his friend off to the temple, the town's people were preparing to see their young wizard off on his journey.

Joey was more ready than ever to enter training. By just focusing his energy, he was now able to perform a much greater variety of everyday tasks with his wand than when Billy met him. Ever generous, Joey continued to let Billy try to use the wand. But every time, just as at the lake, nothing would happen. Billy would become impatient, but Joey was always understanding of the challenges Billy faced.

"The time will come," Joey said, "when you are able to focus all of that energy you have, and something you think of will come true."

On the day of their departure, Mr. and Mrs. McGregor sat with the boys at the breakfast table, as they had done every day since Billy had arrived.

Mr. McGregor drank the last drink of his morning coffee. "Are you sure you want to walk Joey down to the pickup location? It's an awfully long way, and then you will have to turn around and come all the way back by yourself."

"Yes sir," Billy said. "Joey has taught me all about these parts and the way things work around here. I wouldn't let my best friend go off and leave me without seeing him all the way."

"Besides," added Joey. "Billy has been helping me train all this time, and I at least want him to get to see the Journeyman ship."

"Yes, I have to see the Journeyman ship," Billy said. "What's the Journeyman ship?"

"You will see," said Joey, as the whole family laughed at his confusion.

Billy and Joey gathered up the things they had packed the night before. In addition to an extra set of clothes, Mrs. McGregor had made waterlily sandwiches and packed them along with fresh starfruit and dossleberry juice. "Looks like you two are ready to go," said Mrs. McGregor.

The boys said their goodbyes, and after Mrs. McGregor had showered her son with a quite embarrassing amount of hugs and kisses, walked out of the house and down the main street of town. The townsfolk had come out of their shops and homes to wave to the boys and wish them well. Mr. Standish had a big bag of locust honey candy for each of them to eat along the way.

Even old Mrs. Templeton made it down from her home on the hill to give her best wishes. As the boys walked by, she motioned for them to come over. "Remember boys, things aren't always what they appear when you leave the comfort of our little community," she said. "The world is a big place filled with strange things and even stranger people."

The boys nodded as she reached out to grab each of their hands and squeeze them as tightly as a frail old woman could. "Remember," she added, "Keep those you know to be friends closer than your own breath, for those who know your heart the best, can best help protect it."

The boys thanked Mrs. Templeton and walked out of town. They could not have picked a better day to start this journey. The sun was shining and a warm breeze blew through the air. The boys were excited about the two-day walk and a bit saddened as well. They both knew this would be the last time they would spend together for quite a while.

"Hey Joey, what do you think Mrs. Templeton meant about strange things and stranger people," Billy asked.

"The world outside of where we live is not exactly what we are used to seeing. It has people who appear completely unlike we do and of different races," Joey said. "And all the races train in the same temple. The only requirement is the magic within you."

"I would love to see some different people before you head off to your the training ," said Billy. "That would be amazing."

"I'm so excited that the Journeyman ship picks up in the town of Dromel," Joey said. "I've never been there before but from what I have heard it is amazing. There should be quite a few things to see."

"I can't wait," said Billy. "I have never seen Dromel either. In fact, as of a few months ago, I hadn't even seen Turnshire!"

"Our little town is pretty old fashioned and not very advanced compared to the bigger cities, but that's not necessarily a bad thing," Joey said. "Mrs. Templeton always said the reason so few people can use magic anymore is because they have relied too much on other things."

Billy and Joey walked on for hours. They talked about the different things they hoped to see, and Joey tried to explain what he thought the training would be like for him. The temple, as he knew, relied very little on gadgets or technology because the high wizards insisted that if you didn't draw from the power inside you, you would lose it.

As the sun went down, the boys decided it best to set up camp and start a fire for the night. After plenty of wood was gathered, they settled in for a night's rest. Both were exhausted from the long journey and drifted straight to sleep.

In the night, the boys were awakened by loud snarling and growling sounds coming from the forest around them.

"What's that," Billy asked?

"I'm not sure," said Joey. "Let's just keep quiet."

The boys stood next to the fire, quietly listening. As the sounds continued, they began to hear what seemed to be whispering. "That has to be him, it does," they heard a strange voice mumble in the dark. "We have to take that one back, we do," another added.

The boys glanced at each other, not sure if they should run or stay by the safety of their fire. Out from the black woods surrounding them, hideous little creatures slowly emerged. They were very lizard-like but walked on two feet. They had pointed ears, were about three feet tall, and had dark beady eyes. As they walked into the fire's light, they growled and gazed at the boys. One of the creatures was larger than the others, and it raised its clawed hand to point at Billy.

"You will come with us, you will," the creature growled.

"What do you want with me?" Billy asked.

The creature stared back at Billy with its dark eyes. "You will come or we will take!"

Slowly, the little monsters began edging towards them. The frightened boys moved even closer together, and Joey pulled out his wand. "I don't know what to do," he said.

As if in their defense, a cat-like creature quickly descended from the tree branches above them and landed next to the boys. It initially crouched as it landed, then stood tall. The creature held a wand that glowed brighter than the fire.

"Close your eyes!" it said, raising its wand.
"What?" Joey said frantically, "Why?"

"Just trust me! Close your eyes now!" The two boys closed their eyes tightly, and they heard the creature yell "*luminous astrum.*"

From the wand of the cat-like creature flowed a light brighter than the sun. The black-eyed beings surrounding the boys began screaming from the pain that the light caused their eyes.

"Now follow me and stay close!" The cat-like creature took off, running into the dark forest. The boys didn't know what the intentions of this feline sorcerer were, but they did know it beat the alternative.

"Stay right behind me," he said, continuing to run through the pitch-black forest.

How he could see where to run was a mystery to Billy. The dense woods they were traveling through were as black as coal. In exhausted silence, they followed until the sun began to rise and the creature stopped.

"My name is Shadullahan," the creature said in a deep voice, "but you can call me Shadow."

"I'm Joey, and this is Billy. Are you a Cha'tool?" Joey replied, seeing that Billy was too afraid to speak.

"That I am," Shadow said, smiling. "Headed to the temple to train. I followed you two for several miles then decided to sleep upstairs in the trees. Good thing I did, I'd say. What did those imps want you for anyway?"

"Imps?" Billy replied. "I have never seen one of those things in my life."

"Imps are nasty creatures," Shadow said with a frown. "Some say they are little demons left around from when the dark one was in power. Best we stay away from them if we can."

"I agree," said Joey. "My friend Billy here is seeing me off to the Journeyman ship. Want to travel with us?"

"Indeed I would," said Shadow. "I'd be most delighted to."

The three young boys walked on towards the town of Dromel. Shadow told them all about where he came from and about the Cha'tool race. He spoke of how they made their homes in the tops of the trees and how the Cha'tool excelled in support magic. Much like Mrs. Templeton had mastered healing magic, the Cha'tool were masters of support. That style of magic had forged the blinding light spell that helped the boys escape the imps, and also allowed Shadow to see easily in the dark with the night-eye spell.

He told them how his father had been a master of support magic many years ago, but was killed by the dark one when trying to oppose him. He admitted that he considered himself at best a beginner, but hoped to become a master like his father before him through the rigorous training at the temple.

When they arrived at the town of Dromel, they found it to be a bustling place. The streets were lined with shiny lamp posts, and the buildings stretched several stories into the sky. Unlike the wood frame houses they were used to seeing in Turnshire, most structures were made of brick or stone. The people here seemed so busy and caught up in the city's pace that they hardly noticed the arrival of the three strangers, but the young boys certainly noticed them.

One woman was wearing a very odd hat several feet tall that was made of goose feathers. The man walking at her side, most likely her husband, was dressed in a little suit and bore a striking resemblance to a penguin. They high-stepped quite proudly in their attire, their noses pointed sternly in the air.

Those who did look at the boys were focused mostly on Shadow. It was quite apparent that he may have been the first Cha'tool any of the townspeople had ever seen.

"So where do we go?" Billy asked.

"Across town, over to the docks," Joey answered. "Where else would you find a ship?"

They walked through town and to the docks. Posted on the docks' edge was a sturdy wooden sign with letters magically burnt into the board reading:

POTENTIAL STUDENTS OF THE HIGH
TEMPLE WELCOME

"This must be the place," said Joey. "I wonder what time it is supposed to be here exactly?"

As if an answer to Joey's question, the board began to smoke and the letters drifted off in the rising smoke. Appearing in their place was the inscription:

THE NEXT AVAILABLE DEPARTURE TIME IS EXACTLY 3:30

"That's only a few minutes from now," said Shadow as the boys gaped in amazement. "We can just wait, I suppose."

"Well," said Billy staring down at the ground. "I guess this is it."

"I suppose it is," said Joey, reaching out to shake Billy's hand. "Will you make it back okay on your own?"

"I know the way and I will be fine," Billy said. "Thank you so much for everything."

"Here comes the ship!" said Shadow.

Billy turned and looked across the sea. He gazed at the deep blue water as the foam burst from the waves rolling over, but he could see no ship.

"Not there," said Joey pointing at the ocean. "There!"

Joey stretched his hand up to the sky. There, the bow of a ship was amazingly breaking through a large fluffy cloud. It was a massive, multi-decked vessel made of huge timbers of wood. Above it, huge white sails billowed in the steady wind. A flag bearing the picture of a dragon with lightning coming from its mouth was hoisted at the top of the mast.

"Is that the Journeyman ship?" Billy asked. "It's unbelievable!"

The boys watched as the ship slowly descended from the sky and softly set itself into the water at the end of the pier. A drawbridge came crashing down against the dock, creating a walkway onto the ship. Out of the ship walked a very short, stocky man, wearing large leather boots and a heavy brown coat.

"All aboard who's going aboard!" he shouted in a deep voice.

The boys walked up to the man slowly.

"Don't be so scared, kids. I'm a dwarf, not a monster. My name is Nero Celsus and I'm the operator of this fine vessel."

The boys introduced themselves to Nero. This was the first time any of them had seen a dwarf. He was a jolly fellow with coarse red hair and a full, scratchy looking beard. His skin was leathery and his face plump, with cheeks that had been chapped by the wind.

"I've got a few supplies to pick up, but we will be leaving shortly," he said. "It's better to load up now than to get left behind later."

Billy said his final goodbyes to Joey and Shadow, and after watching them load onto the ship he turned and walked back towards the town.

"Why aren't you loading up my boy?" asked Nero.

"Because I can't do magic," Billy replied.

Nero smiled and with a chuckle said, "I have a feeling you don't know what you can do lad… in time… yes in time."

Billy walked off by himself, trying to figure out what it was that Nero meant. He thought about what his friends would be learning and what it would be like for them at the temple. He wondered if they were really ready to manage the studies and training that they were about to encounter. As he walked, lost in his daydreaming, he accidentally walked into a peculiar hooded figure.

"Excuse me," Billy said to the stranger.

"Excuse me," he heard a growly voice say as the shadowy figure looked up.

Under the cloak, he saw the black beady eyes of the imp from the forest. He quickly glanced around and realized this imp was not alone. "You come with us now, you do," the imp said with a snarl.

Billy did the only thing he could—he turned and ran. He sprinted as fast as he could down a side alley, the hisses and snarls of the imps close behind.

As Billy burst from the alley, he saw the ocean before him and the Journeyman several yards away. He turned and raced down the seaside walk without a thought of stopping or looking back.

As he approached the magical ship, he noticed the drawbridge was still lowered. He leapt onto the ship and bounded down a passageway, crashing into Shadow. Both Shadow and Billy fell to the ground from the collision..

"What are you doing?" Shadow asked, startled.

"The imps..." Billy said still catching his breath. "They were chasing me!"

Joey helped Billy and Shadow to their feet. "We have to tell Nero right away!"

"Tell me what?" Nero said, walking up as he tugged on his thick red beard. "What has got you boys so bothered?"

"The imps..." Billy said, still gasping for air. "They were trying to get me... and they still are... and they're right outside the ship!"

"That is completely and absolutely impossible," said Nero.

"No sir," Billy said. "I'm not lying. They really are right outside!"

Nero pointed over to the window of the ship and laughed. "Unless imps have learned to fly," he said. "There will be none of them bothering you or anyone else while we are on this ship."

The boys looked out the window to see billowy clouds racing by as the ship moved silently through the air.

"Oh no, I'm not supposed to be on here," Billy said.

"Nobody gets on this ship, unless they're supposed to be on this ship," said Nero, who was quite amused. "You boys just sit back and enjoy the ride.

Won't be much relaxation going on once the training begins."

Chapter Five
Flying and falling

Traveling on the Journeyman ship was unlike anything the boys had done before.

Though the ship moved through the air at unbelievable speeds, it flew in complete silence. The boys watched the clouds race by and the ground beneath the ship become only a blur.

"Who is flying the ship?" Joey asked.

"Flying the ship?" Nero said. "Why would anyone need to fly the ship?"

The boys looked at each other in astonishment.

"The Journeyman ship needs no pilot," Nero chuckled. "She knows right where she is going, so you boys just relax. We still have quite a few many hours until we arrive at the high temple."

Nero headed off down a hallway, and the boys began to look around. The ship was a huge vessel and yet, to their surprise, they appeared to be the only ones on board. It was finely crafted, made of a dark wood, and had floors so clean you could eat off of them.

"Let's see if we can make our way up to the deck," Shadow said.

The boys walked through the ship, following the same passage in which Nero had left them before. The passageways were long, and the silence was almost eerie and broken only by the sounds of their footsteps.

A little further down one of the hallways, they came to a black spiral staircase. As they approached it, they started to hear a gentle hum coming from above them. The boys climbed up the spiral staircase and onto the open deck of the ship.

What they saw was truly breathtaking. The blue sky above them was filled with puffy white clouds racing by. Brooms, mops, and pails glided effortlessly across the deck, working together with magic to keep everything in tiptop shape without anyone actually using them. Tiny dragonfly-like creatures of every color of the rainbow buzzed about, making little chirping and whistling sounds.

The boys stood there, gazing around in amazement. "Quite a sight, isn't it?" Nero said walking up. "The widdlebugs are hitchhikers, but they don't hurt nothin'."

"Is that what those little creatures are?" Joey asked, pointing at the brightly colored insects.

"Widdlebugs are what they are," said Nero. "There's no better creature for bringing good luck than widdlebugs."

Just as Nero spoke these words, the ship shook violently and tipped hard to the right, knocking the boys and Nero to the ground. The ship leveled out, but then began to shake as it flew.

"What in Atlantis was that?" said Nero, pulling out a large pocket watch.

With the push of a button, the watch sprang open and Nero carefully examined it. "Looks like we got ourselves a dragon wanting to play!" he said.

The ship shook again and a large winged reptile flew by the ship's sails with a sound like the crackling of thunder. The creature was huge, with a body covered with dark, forest-green scales and leathery wings. The beast flew high into the air and seemed to block out the sun as it moved in the sky, casting a heart-chilling shadow across the ship.

The beast spread its giant wings and, turning towards the ship, opened its mouth wide. Fire spewed out, just missing the deck of the ship as Nero and the boys ducked to avoid the heat from the fiery blast.

"Oh no," Nero said, looking up to see one of the sails igniting into flames. "It looks like we will be going down!"

The ship leaned forward with its front sail on fire and began to lose altitude. Nero reached into his pocket and pulled from it a tiny capsule that he quickly threw onto the deck of the ship. The capsule burst into a puff of white smoke, and in its place appeared a large woven basket.

"Get in!" Nero said. "There isn't very much time."

The boys quickly climbed into the basket as the dragon sent another flame burning through the other sail. Once inside, the widdlebugs began to swarm all around them. As the brightly colored cloud of widdlebugs grew denser around them, the insects collectively made a high-pitched whistle.

Joey took out his wand and pointed it up into the blanket of bugs. Immediately, the insects flew straight up into the sky like a colorful tornado and disappeared.

"What did you do?" asked Billy.

"I didn't do anything," said Joey. "They just left."

"The widdlebugs teleported us down to the ground using some sort of magic," said Shadow.

The boys climbed out and looked around the area in which the basket had settled. Burnt, black earth extended beneath their feet in all directions like an ashy starless night. The ground itself was completely scorched and a few smoldering tree stumps was all they could see nearby.

"Where is Nero?" Billy replied. Looking around, they saw no sign of either. The boys quickly searched the sky, thinking they just might see the ship still flying, but it was nowhere to be found. What they did see, however, was the fire-breathing dragon that had been terrorizing them, hovering over the ground in the distance.

"He's looking for us!" Shadow said. "We have to get moving!"

In the distance, they could see a bit of earth still untouched by the flames at the base of a mountain range.

"There," Billy said, pointing to the tree line near the mountains. "We have to get there."

The boys ran towards the mountain as fast as they could. With each step they took, dusty ash stirred from the ground.

"Keep moving," said Shadow. "Let's get there before he spots us."

As the boys reached the tree line, they heard a tremendous roar behind them. Looking back, they saw the dragon violently shaking the basket in his mouth before igniting it into flame.

"That would have been us," Billy said.

After destroying the basket, the dragon began sniffing the ground. It froze in place, lifted its head, and stared coldly at the mountain to which the boys had fled.

"He found us," said Shadow, his voice trembling. "We have to move."

The boys quickly made their way through the sparse trees towards the mountain.

Joey pointed up the hillside. "Up there! We need to get up there!"

Half way up the rocky slope was the opening to a large cave. Going into an unexplored cave didn't seem very smart, but was a welcome escape compared to the possibility of facing down a dragon in the open.

The boys raced up the hillside, stumbling and slipping on the loose rocks. With their legs giving out and their lungs gasping for air, they made it to the entrance of the cave. There, at the entrance, was one lone widdlebug. It hovered there, radiating a rainbow of light.

"What is it doing?" Joey asked as the boys stared at the glowing insect.

"I think it wants us to follow it," said Billy as the widdlebug darted off into the cave.

Behind them, the dragon let out another ear-crushing roar as it reached the tree line. Quickly, the boys raced into the cave. The ground was hard, yet slippery due to the cave's moisture. The light of the widdlebug guided them as it bounced off the cave's cold and grey walls.

The boys ran along, following the luminous widdlebug until they arrived at a large, open area of the cave. As the boys entered the area, they noticed that the stone beneath their feet had changed. The floor of this chamber was covered with golden coins.

Shadow lifted his wand above his head. "*Candeous Consisto!*"

A glowing ball shot forth from the wand and floated to the top of the chamber. Light pouring down from the floating ball filled every inch of the room.

The boys stood still, silenced by what they saw. The room they were standing in was enormous, and golden coins and precious gems covered every inch of it. Valuable treasures were stacked as high as the eye could see.

"You could buy all the locust honey candy in the world with this much gold," Joey said, reaching down to pick up a shiny red crystal and holding the gem to his eye. "Could this all be real?"

"How did it all get here?" asked Shadow, kneeling to look at the treasures more closely.

The little widdlebug darted across the treasure-filled room and headed a few feet down another tunnel.

"I think it wants us to follow him that way now," Billy said, pointing to the tunnel.

"But what are we supposed to do about all this treasure?" Joey asked, picking up a few of the coins.

The widdlebug made a few high whistles and flashed on and off more brightly. The boys looked at one another and back at the treasure, then heard a deafening roar coming from the entrance of the cave.

"Gold and jewels won't do us any good at all if we're not alive to do anything with them," Billy said as they ran for the other tunnel.

As they raced after their widdlebug guide, they heard the dragon crashing through the treasure-filled chamber. The clinking and grinding of thousands of coins under the weight of the dragon echoed in the hallway behind them, but they didn't look back.

After running far enough to no longer hear the sounds of the dragon, the widdlebug's light went out. The boys stopped running and stood as silent and as still as they could.

"Where did the light go?" Billy asked.

"Can you see anything, Shadow?" asked Joey.

Staring off into the darkness, Shadow strained to see the path in front of them.

"I can't see a thing," he whispered, "but we'd better keep it dark and quiet for now.

Reaching out and grabbing hold of one another, the boys slowly and carefully made their way forward. They didn't dare cast a spell to brighten the path for fear that the dragon would see it as well. As they walked silently in the dark, they began to hear the sound of water. The air became thick with foggy moisture.

"There is some sort of light ahead," whispered Shadow.

"Are you sure?" asked Joey. "I can't see a thing."

"There is definitely a light," Shadow replied. "My eyesight has never let me down."

The dampness increased as they walked on until they began to see the faint glow in the distance. As they approached the light, it continued to grow brighter until they walked out of the tunnel into a new chamber that had walls covered with rock that stretched all the way to the ceiling at least ten times taller than any of the boys.

This chamber held no gold, only brilliant blue water that glowed as the boys looked upon it. A few holes in the ceiling allowed light to cascade down into the room and brighten the surroundings. The widdlebug they had been following hovered quietly over the center of a small pool of water in the center of the room.

"What's he doing now?" Joey asked, pointed at the bug.

The widdlebug, hovering above the center of the bright blue water, began making a low-pitched hum that increased steadily. A very faint glow came from the bug and the hum grew increasingly louder.

"It needs to be quiet," said Shadow, "or it's going to let the dragon know where we are."

They heard a deep growl and the clinking of coins coming from the hallway in which they had fled.

"Oh no," said Billy. "He knows where we are."

"Quick," said Shadow. "Help me move these big rocks to block the entrance."

Shadow and Joey used their wands to begin floating them over, sealing off the tunnel.

"Billy, you have to do something about that bug," Joey said as the little creature grew louder and increasingly bright. Billy began to climb the rocky wall, trying to get closer to the bug.

"It's no good," said Billy. "I don't know how to stop him. Maybe we can climb out through one of the holes in the ceiling."

Joey and Shadow lowered their wands and ran to the rocky wall Billy was climbing. The dragon crashed against the blocks the boys had placed against the entrance.

"It's here!" Billy yelled.

The dragon roared and slowly began pushing the rocks from the opening. The horned nose of the beast fought its way into the chamber. As it breathed into the chamber, the smell of rotting flesh filled the air.

Billy, almost to the top of the chamber, looked back to see Shadow not far behind him. His quick and nimble movements allowed him to climb with great ease. Joey however, was not so lucky, and before he had made it even halfway up the wall, the dragon burst into the area.

It stood up tall, leaning out over the water beneath it and looked around. Quickly, the beast spotted Joey struggling to climb the walls and moved towards him.

Still hovering over the water, the widdlebug began to make a high pitched sound that caused the dragon to suddenly writhe in pain. The sound was incredibly loud and the very air seemed to quiver as the beast shook its head violently from side to side.

Through the opening above, a voice yelled down into the cavern. "Can you boys hear me?"

The voice of Nero was very welcome to the scared young men.

"Yes!" Billy said. "We are down here and we need help!" Down the hole came a finely woven rope. It was long and thin and made of a bright silver metal that was somehow soft and flexible.

"I'm dropping a rope in boys," said Nero. "Make sure you all get a real good grip on it."

Billy and Shadow grabbed hold of the rope tightly and tossed the end of it down to Joey, who was now only a few feet behind them.

"Will it hold?" Joey asked, wrapping his hands around the thin shiny rope.

"Of course I can hold it," said Nero, not fully hearing Joey's question.

Nero pulled hard up on the rope, swinging the boys off the wall and out across the water. The boys clung to the rope as they dangled directly over the bright blue pool. The dragon reached out with his massive clawed paw and struck the widdlebug, sending it crashing straight down into the water where it disappeared. The pool began to bubble and churn as the dragon quickly cleared his head, turning his attention to the three boys hanging from the rope.

The beast's eyes were shiny and black, and he stared, breathing on the boys through his massive nostrils. It almost seemed to smile at the frightened children, revealing to them jagged rows of sharp teeth and a large forked tongue.

"Pull us up!" Billy yelled as they swung in front of the beast.

"I'm not sure if I can pull you up," said Nero. "You weigh a bit more than I expected."

"I thought you said you could hold us!" yelled Shadow.

"I'm holding you just fine. It's the pulling you up part that's a bit of a problem."

The dragon opened its mouth and let out another loud roar, this time with a sinister playfulness, clearly thinking it had the boys at its mercy. Its breath alone sent the boys swinging back and forth across the top of the water.

"So what are we supposed to do now!" yelled Joey.

"My best advice to you is to just let go," said Nero. "Just let go."

The water beneath the boys began to bubble wildly and glow brightly. Beneath the surface, you could see the outline of what appeared to be the widdlebug.

"Just let go?" said Billy. "Let go! Are you serious?"

"You could always just hang around here and feed a dragon," Nero chuckled.

Joey had heard enough and decided to take Nero's advice and let go of the rope. He fell down into the water and disappeared beneath the bubbling surface without a splash or sound.

"I guess that's how it works," said Shadow, and following Joey, let go of the rope and vanished beneath the water.

"That's how what works?" Billy yelled.

His brain was telling him to let go of the rope and follow the example set by his friends, but his fear kept him gripping the rope tightly. The dragon opened his mouth, poised to eat Billy in one bite.

"Let go!!!" Nero yelled down to Billy.

The dragon lunged forward with its sharp and jagged teeth. Billy released the rope just before the dragon's jaws could close around him and fell screaming into the water below.

Chapter Six
Welcome to the temple

Still screaming, Billy was surprised to find himself with no need to swim at all. There was no water for his hands to splash through. Instead he found himself tightly gripping a finely trimmed handful of green grass.

Billy looked around to see not only his friends but three other children staring down at him as well. All the children were giggling at the sight of him lying on the grass screaming and trying to swim.

Billy stood up with his heart still racing as he tried to catch his breath. He and the other children were in a large courtyard with every detail of the grounds meticulously in order. Tall buildings like stone castles, several feet high, surrounded the area.

An old robed man with long grey hair stood in front of the children on a wooden stage. Looking at the children, he cleared his voice and in a deep tone said, "Welcome children. I am the high wizard of the realm, Theodorus Dekel. You are all gathered here today, at this very moment, because you have passed your first test. Over the next few years, you will be learning and growing in your magical ability as you never have before. You will be challenged in ways you cannot even begin to imagine, but these challenges are necessary if you are to become one of the keepers of our world and be fully prepared for what awaits you. While each of you comes from a different place, and has a unique background, it is important that you learn to trust and lean on one another, and grow and learn together."

Looking around, Billy could see that there were vast differences among the students.

Shadow was the only Cha'tool present.

Another student was quite reptilian, covered in scales; he stared ahead with large glassy eyes.

There were two other children as well, one boy and one girl, who appeared to be human although very pale-skinned. Each had blonde hair and blue eyes, and seemed to be from the same part of the world.

"Before continuing, I think it is important for you students to meet the ones who will be instructing you," Dekel said, "or have been instructing you, I should say."

Over the walls flew a human-like creature with marvelous wings covered in large silver feathers. It had sharp talons in place of its legs, and moved so fast it was hardly visible. It swooped down just over the children's heads. The students all reached for their wands in defense except for Billy, who wouldn't be able to use one if he had it.

"Easy students, there is no need to be alarmed," said Dekel.

The young pale skinned girl from the other group said, "But sir, that's the same harpy that attacked us earlier!"

"That," said Dekel, "is Persephone Medea, one of your instructors."

The harpy flew onto the stage and transformed into a woman with short brown hair. She wore a grey robe and had in her hand a wand made of a twisted and knotted wood.

"You performed quite well, children," she said as she nodded in approval to the other group of students. "I expect great things from each of you."

The children, still startled by the transformation, reluctantly put their wands away.

"And, though some of you may have already met," said Dekel, "let me introduce to you High Mage Belenos Krishna."

A dark shadow was cast over the courtyard, and as the students looked up, they saw the same black dragon that had terrorized the boys just moments before. The giant beast cupped its wings, and while landing on the platform next to Dekel and Medea, transformed into a tall muscular man. His head was shaved and he stared down at the children, holding a dull black wand.

"Pleasure," Krishna said without changing an inch of the stone-cold expression upon his face.

"That's amazing!" said Joey, looking up at Krishna.

"And last, but certainly not least," said Dekel, "let me introduce to you, Truman Conch."

Up the steps, leading to the stage walked a small skinny man. He looked to be a hundred pounds, maybe less, and his grey robe seemed to swallow him whole. He had small round glasses, and his untidy hair was speckled with grey and white.

"Hello students," he said. "We are going to learn all about each other this year." He laughed in a very high-pitched and unthreatening way and smiled down at the students.

"Unfortunately," said Dekel, "the students that Professor Conch was evaluating did not pass the qualification tests."

"Most unfortunate indeed," said Conch, laughing in the same high-pitched voice. This time the laugh did not seem so innocent.

"Now students," said Dekel, "If you will simply follow your instructors, they will take you to the hall of records and prophecy, which should be able to answer a few more of your questions."

The six students followed the wizards into the castle and down a stone corridor. The passage was lined with statues at every turn. Each statue representing a different creature, ranging from everyday forest animals to mythical creatures Billy had only dreamed about. The eyes of the finely sculpted statues seemed to follow the students as they walked.

"So what is the hall of prophecy?" Billy whispered to Joey as they walked past a large statue of a gryphon.

"The hall of prophecy and records," said Krishna, quite annoyed, "is where the students will be informed."

"Informed?" asked Joey. "Informed about what?"

"Everything." said Conch. "You will be informed about everything that you need to know at this point, nothing more, and nothing less."

The students were led to a large set of oak doors. Conch pulled out his wand, pointed at the center of the doors and said, "*Obvius Publicus.*"

The giant wooden doors creaked as they slowly opened. Inside, hundreds of shelves filled with books of every type lined the massive room.

"This is the ancient library of the magus," said Medea. "Knowledge of the arts, and of the magical Flow, has been passed down for centuries and placed within the pages of these works. You are always welcome in what little free time you will have to visit here and search these records."

Medea continued to walk through the library.

The students gazed at the seemingly infinite selection of books, but stayed close to their instructors. Reaching the far corner of the library, they approached a dull stone wall. The image of a bell was engraved on the wall.

Medea touched the engraving with her wand, and it began to glow. Slowly the glowing image grew until it was as large as the students were and then disappeared, leaving behind a bell-shaped opening large enough to pass through.

"Into this room you must go alone," said Conch.

"What are we supposed to do once we are inside?" asked Shadow.

"It will be made clear," Medea said. "Now in you go."

The students walked into the dark room one after another. As the last student entered the room, the wall closed behind them. They stood there silently.

"*Illuminos*," said the female student as her wand lit the room. "I'm Lilith Ogletree and this is

Warden Fallow," she said, pointing to the light-skinned boy. "Warden doesn't really like to talk very much."

"And you can just call me Scartail," said the lizard-like student.

The boys introduced themselves to their new classmates.

"So what is it we are supposed to do?" said Scartail.

The students illuminated their wands and looked around the room. The stone floor echoed, much like the corridors they had been walking through, and was completely empty except for a little silver bell sitting on a square carved table in the center of the room. It had a very aged wooden handle, its color a dark fading brown.

"I guess it has something to do with this," said Billy, picking up the bell.

He tried to ring it, but it made no sound. The light from the student's wands disappeared completely and everything went black.

"Shine a light over here. There is something wrong with the bell," he said, but looking down, he realized the bell had disappeared.

"Joey… Shadow…" Billy asked in the darkness. "Are you there?"

There was no answer, just the sound of nothing, of darkness. The unlit room was disturbing compared to the excitement exhibited by the children entering this journey with Billy. Then, an illumination in the distance, a place for Billy to move toward. Ahead he saw a large altar. An animal appeared to be lying upon it, but Billy could not make out what animal it was. Behind the altar was a stranger wearing a dark black cloak. He was working with various potions and chemicals and chanting in a language Billy had never heard before.

Billy watched as three wizards dressed in grey, approached the person in the black cloak. The stranger turned, and pointing a wand sent a burst of lightning at the three, striking one of them in the arm. The other two readied their wands and used them to float the man in the black cloak off the ground, then hold him in a captive ball of energy as he continued his chant. The ball of energy swirled and pulsated through a rainbow of light as it drew tighter around the chanting figure. The wizard who had been previously struck by the lightning blast raised his wand and sent a burst of blue light ripping through the captive ball of energy and the black cloak.

Slowly, the blue light faded away, and Billy was left seeing only the bell-shaped light that was the initial entrance to the room. The other students, along with Billy, were lying on the ground trying to make sense of their surroundings. Carefully, they got to their feet and walked out of the room and back into the presence of the three instructors.

"What you just witnessed," said Medea, "was the last time a truly evil force threatened the balance in our world. Three wizards all trained in this very same temple stood side by side against the dark one on the eve of him coming into immeasurable power. Together, these wizards cast him into another plane of existence, never to threaten our world again."

"What was the power he was trying to get?" asked Lilith.

"The power shall not be spoken of because it does not exist anymore," said Conch. "No use wasting your time even pondering it."

"Now," said Medea, "off to exchange your wands for those you will be using for your studies here at the temple."

The students followed the instructors out of the library and through the front gates. Across the grounds, they approached a tall, ancient looking tree. It had no leaves at all, and the bark had weathered away long ago. The large limbs stretched wide, casting shadows down upon the students and the teachers. In the center of the tree's trunk was a hollow opening.

"This is it," said Krishna. "You should all be very excited, very excited indeed! Line up and place your wands in the tree. We haven't got time to waste."

The students lined up in front of the hollowed opening. Lilith was first. As she reached to place her wand inside the opening, the tree suddenly closed around her arm, holding her wand and her hand firmly inside. Lilith screamed and tried to pull her arm from the tree with no success.

"Just relax," said Medea. "Let the Giving Tree do its job."

Lilith stopped struggling and the tree gently opened up, releasing her. The wand she had put into the tree was replaced with one of truly amazing quality. It was solid white with very intricate etchings and smooth as ivory.

The other students followed, each placing their wands into the tree's opening. One by one, they took back wands of amazing craftsmanship, each unique to its owner.

Joey's wand had sharply cut edges and was as golden as the locust honey he had eaten so many times before.

Shadow pulled forth a straight wand that was smooth and polished. It was so black, the light around it seemed to be pulled into its darkness.

One by one, the students exchanged their wands with amazing results, until only Billy remained.

"Well, place your wand in, boy," said Krishna, "you are wasting the others' time."

Billy looked at Krishna, not sure exactly what to say. Not only did he not have a wand, he had never performed anything even resembling a spell.

"Don't just stand there with a stupid look on your face, boy. Place your wand inside the tree."

Billy flushed, then became pale. "I... I don't have one, sir."

"You don't have one?" Krishna said. "What kind of wizard do you think you are if you don't even have a wand?"

"I'm not a wizard," said Billy. "I'm just a boy."

Krishna leaned over and stared face to face with Billy scornfully. "I suppose you are simply here by mistake then. We will have you sent back to your home immediately."

"There are no mistakes," said High Wizard Dekel. "Everyone is here for a reason, though that reason may not be revealed to us just yet."

Dekel reached out and placed his old hand on Billy's shoulder. Leaning down, he whispered into Billy's ear. "Go ahead my boy, place your hand inside the tree."

"But sir... I don't have a wand."

"Just place your hand inside the tree," Dekel said again.

Billy nervously reached his hand into the dark opening of the tree. It felt so cold that his hand actually ached.

"Nothing appears to be happening," said Conch as everyone stared intently at the opening of the tree.

"I told you, sir," said Billy quietly. "I don't have the ability to do magic."

As soon as he said this, the tree began to close around his arm. What once felt freezing cold grew warmer until it was burning hot. All over his hand, it felt like something was moving, as if it was looking for something. The branches of the tree began to shake as Billy closed his eyes and held his breath.

"This can't be good," said Joey, staring up at the tree.

"Have patience, young wizard," said Dekel. "What is to be, will be."

The tree shook for a few more seconds and then suddenly stopped. The hole in the tree opened and Billy removed his hand. He was tingling all over, and as he pulled his hand out was finally able to take a deep breath.

"See, that wasn't so bad," said Dekel with his hand still on Billy's shoulder.

"No sir," Billy said with a trembling voice.

He opened his eyes slowly. In his hand, looking like the small weathered branch of an ancient tree forgotten long ago, he held his very own wand.

"Like I said, everyone is here for a reason," said Dekel.

"Now students," said Medea. "If you will follow me, I will be happy to show you to your quarters."

"And do get a good night's rest," added Conch. "I will be expecting you all promptly at six o'clock tomorrow morning. Don't be late."

Chapter 7
The breakfast buffet

Medea led the students, new wands in hand, back into the temple and guided them down yet another hallway. Remembering how to get from one place to another would be a challenge in itself. After traveling up two flights of stairs, the students came to a hallway neatly labeled THE HALL OF SLUMBER.

Identical wooden doors with shiny brass knobs lined both sides of the hallway. The name of each student was carved into an individual door, and each door was surprisingly the exact color of each newly acquired wand.

"These will be your sleeping quarters," said Medea. "You should find everything you need for your stay here inside your rooms, including your proper dress. Now, off to bed. You will have a very busy day tomorrow."

The students hurried into the rooms to settle in for the night. Each room included a quaint, neatly made little bed, a wardrobe filled with grey robes, a small bedside table, and an empty, heavy wooden trunk. Billy assumed that the robes were the proper training attire, and that the trunk would be filled with whatever belonged there later. Sitting down on his bed, he looked at his wand. It was quite plain compared to the intricate designs of the others that came forth from the Giving Tree, but to him it was the most wonderful thing in the world.

It was made of an old and weathered wood, like that of a cottage that had persisted through the harshness of winter many times. Its handle was a bit larger than the rest of the wand, but seemed to fit perfectly into his hand. He held it tightly and pretended to cast spells with made-up words as he moved it from side to side.

He found his bed to be quite comfortable, and quickly fell asleep with his wand still in hand and with thoughts of what fun adventures the next day would have to offer.

Billy awoke the next morning to a familiar voice and a pounding on the doors.

"Wake up! Wake up!" he heard Nero shouting as he walked down the halls. "Put your robes on, grab your wands, and let's get a move on."

Billy quickly dressed in one of the robes from his wardrobe, and rubbing his eyes, walked out into the hallway.

"So how's it going so far?" Nero asked. "I volunteered to wake you so I could see how all of you were doing."

"Very well so far, I suppose," said Billy as the other students made their way out of the rooms. "I have my very own wand now!"

"We all have new wands!" said Joey, holding his proudly.

"That you do, I see," said Nero. "The Giving Tree has been quite good to the young wizards, quite good indeed."

Each student was dressed in the same grey robes, and all held their new wands proudly for Nero to admire.

"If all are here, and I can see that you are," said Nero, "you can follow me down to the dining area for breakfast and your first lesson of the day."

The students followed Nero down the stairs, through the halls, and into the dining area. Walking in, the students quickly realized that they would eat separately from each other, at their own tables. At each table was a little name card, carefully folded.

"Well, enjoy this morning's lesson kids," said Nero, "and good luck in the rest of your studies."

Nero left the room with the door closing behind him, and the students quickly found their seats.

"This is an interesting way to enjoy a meal," said Joey. "Not very much like home at all, is it?"

Billy started to respond, but as he did, the back door of the room swung open. Into the room floated platter after covered platter, all crafted of the finest silver. Trays, pitchers, plates, and cups whisked through the air in the same manner and laid themselves neatly onto the student's tables. Lastly, in flew white silk napkins that folded themselves methodically into animal shapes and gently came to rest in front of each student.

Conch skipped in with a large smile across his face and positioned himself behind the table at the head of the class.

"Students… I hope that you all enjoyed a good night's rest and are prepared for a most wonderful meal."

Conch raised the lid off the platter at his table, revealing stones of different shapes and sizes. From his pitcher he poured white sand into his cup, and showed the students that his bowl was filled with nothing more than dark soil.

"I know you were probably expecting something a little more pleasant to eat than the items you have before you, but I assure you, your meal will be what you make it."

At that, Conch raised his wand and said "*Mutatio Reformo.*" His bowl of soil was transformed into a steaming bowl of breakfast oats.

Tasting the oats, he breathed deeply and smiled. "Just like I always like them. Here at the temple, you shall be capable of using your magic to even make your meals. Just clear your mind, focus on the taste of the food you desire, point your wand, and say *Mutatio Reformo.*"

As he said it again, his cup of sand transformed into piping-hot dark tea.

He took a sip, then said with a twinkle in his eye, "Students, your time has come...now begin."

Each student focused on their own bowls and plates filled with earthly minerals. Right away, Lilith, Warden, and Shadow had gotten the hang of the transformation spell. Shadow turned his table into a banquet of different fish, birds, and other meats, and was smiling at the feast he had before him.

"Fish... for breakfast..." Joey said, looking rather disgusted by Shadow's preference.

"Fish is great for every meal," said Shadow as he sat down and began eating.

Billy, Joey, and Scartail were having a bit more difficulty with the spell, but after a little more instruction from Conch, Scartail had his meal wiggling before him. Green, slimy goo filled his bowl, and large, bright red worms squirmed on his plate.

"Nothing is better for breakfast than blood worms," he said, slurping one into his mouth.

With a little more practice, Joey had transformed his stones into piping hotcakes covered in sweet syrup.

Billy continued trying his best to cast the spell, but without any luck. Conch adjusted his form and helped with his pronunciation, but no magic took place.

The other students had long finished their meals as Billy continued to try to conjure up even a bread crumb, but again with no results.

"Well class," said Conch. "It is time to move onto the outer grounds for your next lesson of the day."

"What about Billy?" Joey said. "What is he going to eat? We haven't eaten anything since long before we even got on the Journeyman ship."

"Today, the consequences of inability are dealing with hunger. In the future, they could be much, much worse," said Conch. "Now follow me students, and do be sharp!"

The students followed Conch off the temple grounds and deep into the woods. As he walked, he whistled a happy little tune and held his wand high at his chest.

"When walking through parts unknown, students, always carry your wands at the ready."

The students continued to follow Conch down a little stone trail. Out of nowhere, a dog-like creature darted onto the path, and stood growling at the group. With hair raised, it exposed its large sharp teeth and snarled. The students kept behind their teacher. Conch however, hardly moved at all. He simply pointed his wand at the beast and stared deep into its eyes.

"What we have here, students, is a shire wolf, and a beautiful one at that. It's really quite a specimen."

The students watched as the shire wolf slowly closed its mouth, settled its hair, and calmly walked up to Conch. The composed instructor kneeled in front of the beast and gently ran his hands through the shire wolf's mane.

"There are pups nearby," said Conch. "She was only doing what a good mother should. She says she means us no harm at all."

"She said that?" Billy asked.

"Lesson number two is a lesson in basic telepathy," said Conch. "Many spells are cast with the utterance of an incantation, but the use of a wizard's mind goes far beyond that. By focusing your thoughts on connecting with the thoughts of the person or creature you wish to communicate with, you will be able to speak beyond words. This is a mark of every good wizard."

The shire wolf walked off into the woods, and the group continued traveling down the stony trail. Billy was really starting to feel tired after missing another meal, and while the peaceful walk would normally have been quite pleasant he found himself struggling to stay up.

Eventually, the students arrived at the base of a tower. It was obviously very old, and the rock steps spiraling up and around it were covered with green mosses and plants.

"Your next lesson can be found at the top of Cloud Shadow Tower. Now off you go," directed Conch.

Step by step, the students climbed the tower. Before long, they began to feel in their burning legs just how long of a journey it would be to the top. No one was feeling it more than Billy, who without breakfast, was struggling to take even simple steps.

"Let's stop and rest a bit," said Joey, seeing Billy struggling to catch his breath.

Billy stopped and leaned against the rocks. "No, you guys just go on ahead without me."

"We will wait for you," said Shadow, as the other three students continued to climb.

"I won't make you two miss out or even fall behind because of me," said Billy. "Go ahead without me and I will catch up after a short rest."

Joey stared up in the direction of the top of the tower. "You sure?"

"Positive! I will follow you in a bit."

The rest of the class continued up the tower while Billy rested. The top of the climb led them beyond the clouds and onto a rather ordinary platform. For the amount of effort required to reach the summit, it was really quite plain.

Around the edges of the summit were large stone pillars with odd symbols. These pillars formed a circle about a grey table. Above the table, a hole in the ceiling (about the same width as the table) allowed a bit of sunlight to trickle through. Out of the tower, they could see the tops of the white billowy clouds with an occasional grey tint that seemed to stretch to all corners of the kingdom. Medea was waiting, dressed in her familiar grey robe, like that worn by all the professors.

"It appears that we are missing someone," she said, looking at the exhausted students.

"Billy," Shadow said. "He was having a hard time making it up the steps."

"Then all the students must be forced to wait," said Medea, crossing her arms with a frown on her face.

"Can we just start without him?" asked Scartail. "He doesn't have what it takes to be a wizard anyway."

"Mr. Scartail!" said Medea scornfully. "Neither you nor any other person here shall be the judge of who does or does not have what it takes. We will wait!"

Medea and the students waited atop the tower for over a half an hour. The entire time, Medea did not move, gazing straight ahead with her arms still crossed. Eventually, Billy made it to the top of the tower, drenched in sweat and gasping for breath.

"I am glad you decided to join the rest of your class," said Medea. "Now we can finally begin."

"I'm sorry," said Billy. "This morning I didn't get breakfast and I..."

"No excuses, just results," Medea interrupted. "Now class, today you will be working on your ability to communicate using only your mind. This is an ability all good wizards have. In fact, some with no other magical ability at all can do it as well.

"To communicate using only your mind, you must be able to do what is represented on each of these pillars. The symbols you are seeing are translations of ancient languages, and their symbols for focus."

Medea pointed her wand off the platform and the symbols began to glow faintly.

"The ability to communicate with the simpler creatures is a good place to start," she said as a high pitched sound radiated from her wand.

At that moment, a large eagle landed next to one of the pillars. It looked at the children with curiosity, showing no alarm or fear. Other eagles landed on the tower one by one, each positioning itself next to a different pillar. Each eagle was truly magnificent, with finely groomed feathers and a noble expression.

"Today, you will be using your powers to communicate with these amazing creatures," Medea continued as the whistling stopped. "You simply need to clear your minds and focus on the animal's thoughts.

You must first be ready to hear the animal before you can communicate with it.

"To complete this lesson, you must have an eagle fly down and retrieve a single lilycup flower. They grow in abundance this time of the year, but the eagle has no motivation to bring it here other than helping you. Choose your thoughts wisely, and best of luck. One hour is all the time you have to complete this assignment, and have your flower placed on the stone table. You may begin."

The students each stood in front of an eagle and hastily began trying to convince the bird to gather the flowers. Lilith's eagle left almost at once with a wave of Lilith's ivory wand, flying off and returning with a blooming lilycup. Lilith put it on the table and began petting her eagle's soft white feathers.

Before long, all the students had retrieved their flowers except for two. Scartail's eagle had left a good while ago but was yet to return. Billy's eagle was still atop the tower, staring back at him. It was hard to tell if Billy or his eagle was more confused.

"It would appear that a couple of our students are having some trouble communicating with their new feathered friends," said Medea. "Lilith, what is it that

110

you told your eagle, that it would retrieve your flower so quickly?"

"I just told her how beautiful of a creature she was, and that it would help me a great deal if she would be kind enough to return the flower to me," Lilith said, smiling.

"And you, Shadow?"

"I told to the eagle that I would tell him where a stream full of fresh fish was located. I smelled the stream full of fish when we were walking up the trail on our way to the tower."

"And you, Scartail? Why is it that your eagle is still yet to return? What did you say to this noble creature?"

"I told him to bring a white flower back to me and to do it quickly... or I would have to break his wings."

Medea frowned. "It appears your direct approach, and very primitive one I might say, was not the best choice for this situation... not very effective at all. Billy, did your eagle give you any reason as to why it wouldn't fly down for you? Any reason at all?"

"I don't know, professor... I can't hear it saying anything," Billy said, disappointed.

"Well then," said Medea. "We will assume that it is not hearing you either. As for the rest of the students who completed this task effectively, your efforts shall be rewarded. Please step up onto the stone center table."

The other students stepped up onto the stone table in the center of the pillars. With a wave of Medea's wand, they were gone, vanished into the air.

"For completing the tasks effectively, those students now find themselves back at the temple. For not completing the task effectively, you two shall walk down the tower... together!"

With that, Medea disappeared. Billy's eagle flew off into the sky, and the two boys were left standing alone.

"This is unbelievable!" said Scartail. "I have to walk all the way down this tower with a wannabe wizard who has *no* magical ability whatsoever!"

"Don't think I like it any better," said Billy.

The two boys started walking down the steps. Scartail walked quite quickly, almost like he was testing Billy to see if he would be able to keep pace. Billy's legs throbbed with pain, but he wouldn't dare let Scartail know about his discomfort, so he painfully kept up with the reptilian lad.

"I wonder why you are even here," said Scartail.

"I don't think I know for certain either. I guess I was at the right place at the right time."

"You mean the wrong place at the wrong time! Do you have any magical ability at all? Have you ever even done any magic?"

"No," said Billy quietly.

"Then do everyone a favor," said Scartail as he stopped and turned towards Billy, "and just quit! Everyone has worked hard their whole life to get this opportunity, and you come along and make it a joke! Your very presence here mocks our training."

"Do you even know why they call me Scartail?"

"No... I do not," Billy said.

"In my tribe, you don't become a man by simply growing up. You train hard and learn from the other Reptilius people. After your father has decided you have learned enough, have mastered your skills enough, you are sent out into the wilderness to complete your rite of passage. To prove your worth, you must come back with the horn of a rampar, or you don't come back at all. I came back with the horn, but also with this injury to my tail. It was the elders who gave me the name Scartail. It is a name of honor and a symbol of my becoming a warrior.

"Others hold precious the values of honor, hard work, and what the temple represents. You should have enough courage to quit and allow those who deserve to be here the opportunity to move forward without your ignorance holding them back."

The rest of the walk back to the temple was silent.

Billy thought about what was said. There was a big part of him inside that knew much of what Scartail said was right. He had never done anything magical, and he really didn't see how it would be possible for him to learn.

Joey, Shadow, and the other students had spent their whole lives preparing for this, and because he simply ran onto a ship out of fear, it shouldn't give him the right to have the same opportunity.

When they arrived back at the temple it was well past dark. Professor Krishna was waiting at the gates with an expression of disapproval.

"Failure is not acceptable," he said. "It never has been acceptable, and it will never be acceptable. Now, off to your quarters for the night!"

Chapter Eight
Time to quit

Billy felt terrible. It was beginning to be very obvious to him that he was not cut out to be a wizard. Not only did Scartail make it very clear to him that he wasn't welcome, but the professors were obviously very disappointed by his lack of magical ability.

Back at his room, he decided the best thing he could do for everyone was simply to tell Professor Dekel that he was quitting. After gathering up his few belongings in his room, and changing out of his robes, he knocked on Joey's door to tell him the news.

"What? It's only been a couple of days," Joey said. "You can't quit yet."

"No… it's the best thing for everyone," Billy said. "I never had magical abilities, and the rest of you have been doing this all your lives."

Joey grabbed Billy's arm. "But just give it a little more time!"

Billy opened the door and began to walk out. "No, I've made up my mind. I'm on my way to meet with Professor Dekel right now. I'll see if he will send a letter to your parents letting them know that I will be coming."

"That reminds me," Joey said. "Nero dropped off a letter to you earlier. I said I'd be sure that you got it."

Joey pulled a letter out of his drawer and handed it to Billy. Billy's eyes moved back and forth over the letter, and as he read a frozen expression came over his face.

"What's it say?" Joey asked.

"It's from Professor Dekel. He wants to meet with me tonight."

"Well, you were going to speak with him anyway, weren't you?" Joey asked.

"No... he wants to meet with me... on top of Cloud Shadow Tower!"

Climbing the tower the first time was one of the most miserable experiences of Billy's life. Now, with his stomach empty and legs aching, he was being asked to climb it again without any desire to be at the temple, and certainly not the tower.

"What are you going to do?" Joey asked. "You can't leave Professor Dekel waiting for you all night."

"Well, at least this will be the last time I ever have to walk up that stupid tower."

Billy turned and walked out of the temple and down the stony road towards the tower. He thought about how exactly he would tell Professor Dekel he was quitting, and what the old wizard might say to him. He didn't want to let anyone down, but his presence was holding back the others. As he arrived at the base of the tower, his legs were already hurting so bad he could hardly walk.

Looking into the dark night, he could see nothing but blackness towards the top of the tower.

Slowly he began walking up, step by step, each step a little more difficult than the previous one.

Halfway up the tower Billy's legs could carry him no farther. He collapsed onto the stairs and everything faded away.

In his dreams, he began to see a light that flickered vibrantly and made the same little buzzing sound he had heard from the widdlebug. He tried to stand up to follow it, but he couldn't find the strength. The little bug flashed with encouragement, but it was no use.

Billy, laying there with everything drifting away from him, heard a familiar voice.

"Stand up my boy... stand up I say... You have the strength within you!"

I can't do magic... I'm weak... I'm not like the others.

"You are the person that you intended to be my friend... and in you there is power... Now stand up!"

Billy opened his eyes and pulled himself to his feet. Tired and sore, he put one foot in front of the other and made his way up the steps.

When he arrived at the top, he was amazed at what he found, *nothing!* Professor Dekel was nowhere to be found among the stone pillars and center table.

Billy screamed at the top of his lungs. "What is it that you want from me? It's not fair! I have worked and I have done everything that I can! I don't have it in me! I'm not like the others! I'm just a normal kid!"

The center table began to spin slowly, and he heard a quiet voice from above say *get on*.

Billy stood on the table as it slowly rotated, then elevated, lifting Billy gently through the hole in the ceiling. Billy was greeted by a visual wonder. Fountains sprayed water over his head, creating a glass-like dome. Widdlebugs danced in circles around the showering ball as the light shimmered in the water. The four white flowers the eagles had returned stood on the different sides of the platform, soaking up the running water.

Professor Dekel stood, admiring the display.

"Quite an incredible sight, isn't it Billy?" he asked in a quiet voice.

"Yes sir... it really is."

"So... you think you are just a normal little boy, do you? What is 'normal,' anyway?"

"I just mean I don't have the ability to do magic, sir. I don't have it in me."

Dekel smiled and put his hand on Billy's shoulder.

"Look at this amazing display before you child. Just a few hours before, you were within feet of it and you didn't even know it existed. If I hadn't invited you up here, you may never have known."

Dekel reached up into the air and a bright red widdlebug landed on his finger.

"Amazing creatures, they are. Though they are small in size, they understand something that even you can't wrap your mind around at the moment."

"Something I don't understand?" Billy asked.

"Yes, you Billy," Dekel said as he smiled. "The flow of magic takes place in all living things, from the giants of the Pelosian fields, right down to creatures as small as widdlebugs. It is in the plants and trees, the animals of the land, and the birds of the air, and Billy... it is in you."

"Then why can't I do magic like the other students? I try so hard, but still nothing happens!"

Dekel walked closer to Billy.

"For some, it takes years to unlock their ability. Others spend a lifetime trying, and some just need that little spark. They just need a push in the right direction."

"I don't understand sir," Billy said. "A push?"

"See all of this water around you," Dekel said. "This is no ordinary water. It holds something much, much more."

With a wave of Dekel's hand, a drinking cup appeared. Kneeling, he filled the cup and held it out to Billy.

"I, like the other professors and great wizards of the past, journeyed here before and drank from this mysterious fountain. It has an incredible way of unlocking the flow of magic within us."

Billy stared at the water with his eyes wide and full of wonder.

"This is why I brought you here Billy," said Dekel. "Take, drink, and unlock the true power that is within you."

Billy took a long drink of the water. It was cold, and after climbing the tower for a second time in a day it seemed to rejuvenate not only his body but his spirit as well.

"Thank you, sir. I don't know what else to say."

"Then say nothing my boy. Just go out tomorrow and use what you now know you have within you. Let no gift go to waste."

With that, Dekel waved his wand and Billy was transported back to his room.

Billy stood for a moment looking at his hands. He felt different now, almost as if something inside of him had been brought to life. He lied down on his bed and quickly fell asleep.

The next morning, he was the first to wake and was already standing in the hall when Professor Krishna came to gather the students.

"Up early are we, Mr. Huddle?" Krishna said. "Having nightmares, I assume."

"No sir. I'm just trying to be more prepared."

After Krishna had pounded on the other students' doors, they quickly filed out into the halls and followed him down to the dining area. Tables were already set with the dishes neatly filled with sand, rock, and soil that waited to be transformed into the morning breakfast.

"I assume no explanation is needed as to how your meal is to be prepared," said Krishna.

The students stood behind each of their tables. Joey leaned over and whispered to Billy, "Glad to see you didn't quit. I'm going to sneak some of my breakfast out for you to eat, ok?"

"*Mutatio Reformo*," Billy said, pointing his wand at his table.

The dishes before him were transformed into a small mountain of warm food and a bubbling beverage.

"Wow!" Joey said. "What's that?"

"Cheeseburger, fries, and cherry cola," Billy said as he sat down and began eating. "This is the best food I have ever eaten," he said, taking a bite out of his burger.

The other students transformed their breakfast and sat down to enjoy their meals.

The water really worked, Billy thought.

"Yesterday, some of you performed adequately," said Krishna. "Today, Professor Dekel has decided that there will be an award for the student who accomplishes the challenges in the most effective manner. That reward shall be this."

Krishna held up an amulet with a green crystal hanging from it.

"This is an amulet of intercession. It is said to provide its wearer help in a time of need by completely focusing and magnifying his or her magical ability. No one knows the full extent of its power, but it is indeed a rare and ancient artifact."

Krishna placed the amulet into a leather pouch. "It is a truly valuable prize to be won. Now students, follow me and do not dawdle!"

Krishna led the students to a giant room with thousands of pictures on the walls. Each picture was of a different creature.

The animals pictured were not frozen in time, but alive and moving within the pictures.

"This is known as the wall of windows," Krishna said. "These are not merely pictures hanging on the wall, but portals through which we can observe every known creature on the planet. Today's first challenge shall be in the art of transfiguration. Watch closely."

Krishna then turned and faced a picture displaying a ferocious cat-like creature. The animal was much like a tiger in size and shape, but covered with small black scales instead of fur.

"This, students... is a bastet cat."

The animal in the picture walked slowly, crouching low to the ground and stopping every few moments to sniff the air.

"It is important to focus your mind and your energy on what it is that the creature is feeling. You must align your magical center with the Flow that makes the creature what it is. See its hunger and feel its desire."

They watched as it stealthily and silently moved, and then with a burst of speed, lunged forth, springing all of its ferocity on a small defenseless deer. The bastet cat sunk its teeth deep into the creature, killing it instantly.

"*Mutatio Creatura,*" they heard Krishna say, and when they turned, they saw the bastet cat itself standing where Krishna once was. The creature snarled as the students reached for their wands in fear. Rearing onto its hind legs, the creature stood as it transformed back into Krishna.

"That students, is how the transfiguration spell is performed. This is the spell you must master to succeed at today's first lesson."

"Awesome!" said Joey.

"Make that double awesome for me!" said Billy.

"As you all should know by now, a true wizard is only as brilliant as his mind enables him to be," said Krishna "Your mind must not limit you! Each of you shall be given a riddle to solve in order to identify the creature that *you* will become for this challenge. The first student to transform into the correct creature shall be the winner. You may begin."

A small white card appeared in front of each student on the ground. Picking the cards up, the students quickly began to read their given riddles.

Billy's riddle said:

Move of light, in groups do roam,

Across the plains, no place called home,

Ever moving, day and night,

Fleet of foot and glow of stripe

Billy knew right away that this was an ixion, one of the most amazing creatures Old Man Richardson had told him about. It was hard to believe that he once thought them to be imaginary.

He scanned the endless pictures as quickly as he could for the sight of a horse-like creature with glowing stripes. Near the top of the wall, he spotted a herd of them running across an open field. He pointed his wand toward the picture and tried to think about the details of the stories he had once heard. He remembered how the ixions lived for the freedom they felt running across the field, and about how the smell of sweet clover always followed where they passed.

Billy took a long step back away from the wall. "*Mutatio Creatura,*" he said as he stood with his arm stretched forth.

Scartail laughed, "Will you never give up? Breakfast was nothing more than beginner's luck."

"It was a good try," said Joey.

Billy kept his wand on the picture, and his mind focused on the ixion herd. An electric tingle raced up his spine. Smelling the actual scent of clover, he transformed into a large ixion buck. Billy sped around the room in a flash, imitating the blur of the fast-running herd, and then quickly transformed back into himself.

"That is amazing!" said Shadow. "I didn't know those creatures really existed. I thought they were only stories of the elders."

"Very few still do exist," said Krishna. "But that is the correct transformation. Very good, Mr. Huddle."

The rest of the students proceeded to solve their riddles and perform their transformations.

Shadow was the second to transform. He became an eagle, much like those on the top of Cloud Shadow Tower.

Scartail was third, becoming a tamper viper from the Sarluvian Swamps.

The other three students quickly followed, with Lilith becoming a tree ape, Warden a small poodle-like creature called a lolly pup, and Joey a Rainbow Scarab Beetle.

Krishna stood with his arms crossed looking at the students with the same scornful stare on his face. "It appears that each of you performed... acceptably."

Krishna glanced over at Billy. "One of you might even have survived if this was an actual encounter with a darker element and not just simple practice."

Billy smiled from ear to ear. It was nice to be the one moving ahead and not holding the others back.

"Don't get cocky, Mr. Huddle. I said might, not that it was likely," said Krishna. "For your last challenge of the day, Professor Conch will be evaluating the ability to adapt one's skills to the problems presented in a live environment. Let us just say that Professor Conch's previous students did not fare very successful in his evaluation methods. Let's hope you have truly grown in your ability, or it could be very ugly indeed."

Krishna turned and walked to the door exiting the room.   "But first, off to the dining hall. You will have two hours to rest and recover before facing what I can assure you will be your most difficult challenge yet."

The students made their way to the dining area. In place of the usual soil and sand was an amazing display of unique foods and drinks. Meats, breads, fish, exotic desserts, and of course Joey's hotcakes were laid out beautifully at each student's table.

"I guess they decided to be nice and give us food instead of testing us with it," said Billy.

Shadow took a long drink of a warm milky beverage.

"But it makes me even more nervous about how difficult the next challenge will be," he said. "What do you think Conch did to get rid of the other students during the entrance evaluation?"

"I don't have a clue, and I'm not sure I'm ready to find out," said Joey. "For now, I just want to enjoy my meal and try not to think about it. No use stressing over something I don't have control of. These hotcakes, on the other hand, I can control," he said taking a bite.

"I'll eat to that," said Billy.

Chapter Nine
Smile for the birdie

After eating their fill, the students sat around the dining area with millions of questions running through their heads.

What was the next challenge going to be?

What did Krishna mean about adapting one's skills to the problems presented in a live environment?

For the moment, Billy didn't have any skills he could think of, unless he was to feed a cheeseburger to something long enough for him to run away as an ixion.

"What do you think Conch transformed into to get rid of the other students?" Joey asked.

"Maybe a giant serpent… or a sabre beast," said Lilith. "The harpy that we had to face was incredibly nasty. I can't imagine anything worse than that."

"Try a giant black dragon with razor-sharp teeth and professor Krishna's breath," chuckled Joey.

"Dragons may be large, but reptiles are easily understood," said Scartail as he slurped down a juicy blood worm.

Scartail maintained his glare as the other students laughed at his thoughts on reptiles since he was one himself.

"Conch doesn't really seem like a very threatening wizard, does he?" asked Billy.

"No, he does not," said Shadow, getting to his feet. "That is exactly why he is probably the most dangerous of them all."

A loud thump came from the heavy door and Nero suddenly entered. He was trying to catch his breath and was tugging nervously at his coarse beard.

"Conch...," he said, trying to compose himself. "For your next challenge, you have to perform against Conch."

"We know," said Billy. "They told us that after the last test."

"You may know that Conch is involved, but I don't think you know what that means," said Nero. "Be careful and be sure to remember that things are not always what they appear."

"We will Nero," said Joey. "We have already learned a lot."

"Hear what I say young wizards," said Nero. "Conch will surely know your heart by the end of this task. He will know it well, and your mind too. He is a very crafty wizard indeed. Just watch out for yourselves. I want you all back in one piece."

"In one piece?" Shadow asked.

"O, fiddle d' twiddle," said Nero. "I've already said far too much. Just follow me down to the courtyard kids. Your next task will begin there."

The students followed Nero down to the courtyard where Professor Medea and Krishna were waiting for them. There were also six stone chairs arranged in a circle around a low, steady fire.

"If you would, students," said Medea. "Please have a seat in one of these chairs."

Billy and the others cautiously sat and awaited instruction.

"As your final challenge for today, you will be using these channeling chairs to transport yourselves to another place," Medea said. "Make ready your wands, for the challenges that await you shall assess the very fears inside your hearts."

"The challenge for each of you is to acquire a feather from the legendary Symphalian Bird," said Krishna. "Upon doing so, or if you are rendered incapable of continuing, you will be transported back here for review."

"Now students, stare at the fire and allow your minds to focus solely on the flame in front of you," said Medea. Krishna began saying an incantation under his breath and pointing his wand at the fire, whose flames blurred in a blinding, brilliant red and black.

Billy closed his eyes to shield them from the light. When he opened them, he found himself in a strange new place. The pleasant courtyard, his friends, and the instructors were all gone. A dense jungle grew all around him and it appeared to be shaking.

As Billy took a deep breath, the heavy heat and humidity of his surroundings became apparent, and the smell of sulfur was in the air. Hearing a loud boom, Billy looked up to see that he had been transported to the base of a very active volcano. Smoke poured from within it, as the thunderous crashing sounds continued.

From the look of this volcano, it was getting more dangerous by the minute.

"Joey!" he yelled. "Shadow! Is anybody there?"

There was no response. Hearing a loud screech high above, he lifted his eyes to regard what had to be the largest bird in the world. Measured wing to wing, this bird would be more than 20 feet across. Its beak was long and made of bronze, as were its enormous feathers. Soaring high into the air, the creature eclipsed the sun and then dove straight into the thunderous volcano.

You've got to be kidding, Billy thought. *I'm supposed to go in there?*

Billy sat down to think about how he was supposed to get a feather from such an intimidating beast. How could he possibly get inside an active volcano... and once inside, what then?

He decided he could sit around all day and night and still not have an answer, so he might as well do something productive. Reluctantly, he got up and started walking towards the opening at the top of the volcano.

He tried to think about what Nero had told the students.

What did he mean, "things weren't always what they appeared"?

Before long, he came to a steep chasm that kept him from getting any closer to the volcano. Looking into the giant canyon, it appeared to extend straight down and stretch on to the left and the right for miles.

"You wants to get across?" he heard a small, childish voice ask behind him. "You would have to be a silly head to want to go closer to the firespitter."

Billy turned around to see a very young child standing behind him. He had dark brown skin and was dressed in spotted animal hides. As the child pulled on his long, dirty black hair and shuffled his bare feet, a smile crept across his face.

"Hello," said Billy. "Are you from around here?"

"I'm Pumjab," said the boy. "So very lost...so very lost."

Billy walked closer to the boy. "So, you are lost?"

"Pumjab not lost," said the boy. "Pumjab has lost his Moxi. Could you help Pumjab find his Moxi?"

"Your Moxi," Billy asked. "What is a Moxi?"

"Moxi is a small little fluff ball, my daddy says," said Pumjab. "He says he isn't good for nothing, but he is me fluffiest friend in the whole wide world."

A sad expression came across Pumjab's face.

"I got very mad at Moxi for getting in Mommy's clothes and he ran far away. I'm not so mad anymore. I just want to finds my Moxi and make sure he is safe. I'm very worried. You help?"

Billy started to walk away. "I really don't have time to look for your pet," said Billy. "I have too..."

"Please!!!" said the little boy. "It won't be taking long, and I will be crying if I don't find him."

Pumjab's face grew bright red, and his eyes began to swell with tears. He sat down on a log and began to sob uncontrollably.

"Okay," said Billy. "I will help you look, but just for a little while."

Immediately, Pumjab stopped crying and jumped to his feet, searching for his tiny pet. In bushes, up trees, and under logs, the two searched for the fluffy little creature with no luck.

"Are you sure your Moxi is out here in the jungle?" asked Billy.

"There he is!" said Pumjab, pointing down into the canyon. "Down there!"

Several feet down the rock was a little rope bridge extending to the other side. Halfway across, suspended on the swinging ropes, was an eight-legged spider about the size of a baseball. He was covered in long yellow hairs and holding on tightly with all eight limbs.

"That's your Moxi?" said Billy, staring down into the canyon.

"Yes," said Pumjab. "Me Moxi looks ever so scared, he does. Can you save me Moxi? Please!!!"

Billy took a deep breath and climbed carefully down. The walls were rough, but he didn't have much trouble finding his footing and grabbing hold of jutting rock formations within the canyon.

Reaching the little rope bridge, Billy found it to be far less stable than the wall he had just climbed down. He inched his feet slowly across the bridge, with both hands firmly grasping the single slender rope that made up the railing. As the wind blew through the canyon, the little bridge swayed back and forth in the breeze.

"Just don't look down," said Pumjab from above. "It's not that much farther."

Billy couldn't help but do the one thing he was told not to. He looked down! His body got stiff and he froze as the sweltering breeze shifted the tiny ropes. Looking up, he could see the little fluff ball moving slowly away from him.

"Come on little guy. I'm trying to help you," Billy said. "Stay still."

The little creature inched backwards, and Billy continued moving towards it. Moxi made a soft cooing sound as it steadily crept away. Before long, Billy had followed the little spider all the way to the other side of the cavern.

The little insect scuttled into an opening and hurried towards the interior of the mountain. Billy ducked his head and moved into the hole. As he inched forward, he felt the air around him grow increasingly hot. He began to see a warm glow as the temperature continued to increase. Making his way out of the tunnel, Billy looked down to see beneath him a pool of molten lava.

"*I've made it into the volcano,*" he thought.

The little yellow creature dashed back down the opening he had crawled from, disappearing from sight. Billy could see the red bubbling lava and feel the intense heat upon his face. Standing up on the crumbling edge, he looked around.

An enormous nest set on a rocky ledge at the opposite side of the volcano, several feet above him. The nest wasn't made of twigs and sticks. Instead, this massive construction was made of rock and stone. Billy saw the only thing that he needed at this point on the far side of the huge nest, a large bronze feather. With it, he could prove to his professors, the other students, and especially to himself that he did belong at the temple.

With no bird in sight, he started moving carefully around the outer edge. With each step, the crumbling walkway around the volcano's interior became narrower. Slowly and methodically, he made his way to the nest. Using every bit of strength he had, he pushed a large rock aside, allowing him to enter.

The stone tumbled into the lava below and sank swiftly in its burning brew.

Once in the nest, he realized it did not just hold stone and feather. Four large, golden eggs shimmered in the reflecting light of the volcano. Billy reached down to touch one of the precious eggs, but was knocked to the ground by a deafening noise from above.

Looking up, he saw the enormous bronze bird flying into the volcano. Its metallic wings crackled with every flap, and a blinding light reflected off of them. Gazing down, it quickly noticed its eggs were not alone.

The enormous bird tucked its wings and dove straight for the nest. Just before landing, it cupped its wings, sending a rush of air that pushed Billy against the rocky edge. It then opened its giant beak and screeched angrily at Billy.

Inside its beak, Billy could see rows of sharp dagger-like teeth made of the same bronzed metal. He grabbed his wand and pointed it at the bird while inching further away from the golden eggs.

"Professor Conch," Billy said pleading. "Please don't hurt me! I give up. I give up!"

The bird turned, looking intently at the eggs, then back at Billy.

"I didn't touch them, sir. I don't want them at all!"

The bird screeched once more, and with a deft jerk of each wing, shot two razor-sharp feathers at Billy. One just missed him and the other cut his upper arm, leaving a nasty gash.

The bird inclined its head back, then thrust it at Billy. Jumping out of the way, Billy rolled across the ground towards the edge of the nest.

"Please stop... please... stop!"

Billy could think of nowhere else to go, except to tumble into the hot lava. Once more, the bird thrust his large beak at him. Billy grabbed one of the loose feathers lying next to him. With both hands, he struggled to hold the giant metallic feather in front of his face to block the creature's deadly blows.

"Well done my boy, well done indeed," he heard Professor Dekel say.

Billy lowered his makeshift shield and looked around to see all the other students around him, staring in surprise.

"How in the world did you manage to get that?" Joey asked.

Billy dropped the large feather to the ground with a loud thud.

"I have no idea," Billy said. "I thought Professor Conch was going to kill me for sure."

"Well now," said Professor Dekel. "After much discussion with the other instructors, it seems we have declared a winner for today's challenges."

"Yes indeed," said Medea. "For complete mastery and precise application of the *mutatio creatura* spell... and for being the only student who successfully returned the thunderbird's feather... the winner of today's challenge is Billy Huddle."

The other students clapped in recognition as Medea motioned for him to go to the front.

"And with today's successful application of sound magical principles," she said. "Mr. Huddle is awarded the amulet of intercession."

Krishna placed the amulet holding the shiny green stone around his neck. It shimmered in the light of the setting sun as Billy admired it.

"Tonight students, you have all earned a relaxing evening, free of lessons and responsibilities.

Please enjoy it for these times are few," said Professor Dekel.

Professor Dekel nodded to Billy in approval. As the students walked off towards the temple, Billy found Mr. Conch standing on the side.

"Professor Conch," Billy said quietly. "Thank you for not hurting me badly."

"Hurting you badly?" Conch replied. "Why... however did I hurt you at all?"

Billy pulled back the sleeve of his robe, showing the gash the feather had made. It wasn't too severe, but it was definitely noticeable.

"Ouch," said Conch. "Appears that may leave a bit of a scar. Now I suppose we will have something in common."

Conch pulled back his sleeve to reveal a rather large scar on his own arm. "Now how is it you think I was the one that gave you your injury, young wizard?"

"When you shot those sharp feathers at me sir... one cut me a bit... but it's okay now," Billy said.

"I didn't shoot any feathers at you child," Conch chuckled. "Did you think I was the Symphalian bird... or as most call it, the thunderbird?"

"Well… yes sir… weren't you?"

"No, no, no, not at all. I wouldn't set foot near that giant creature, much less turn into it. It is a nasty beast for certain. I was the little boy! Thanks ever so much for helping me find me Moxi," he said with a wink. "Now off you go, Mr. Huddle. Enjoy your evening. Your magic is growing quite strong."

Billy walked back up the stairs to his quarters. He may have enjoyed the library or some other magical room, but all he wanted at the moment was to rest.

As he walked, he thought about how much better he had become at magic. Before, he hadn't been able do anything resembling a spell, and now he was surprising himself. But was it fair?

The other students had spent years training just to qualify for the right to be at the temple. He saw how much time Joey put in practicing and honing his skills, and the challenges that the others had to face. Was it right for him to receive an award for being the best when his ability came from a magical drink and not from within?

Lost in thought and turning a corner on the second floor hallway, Billy walked right into Professor Dekel.

"Daydreaming a bit, are we Billy?" said Dekel. "Very good work today. Very good work indeed."

"Thank you sir," said Billy. "I actually wanted to speak with you about that if you had the time."

"Is that so? I thought you may," said Dekel. "But first if you would, please follow me."

Billy followed Dekel to a large room with a towering ceiling. On the walls hung the portraits of men and woman all wearing robes of different styles and colors. Though all were similarly dressed, it was obvious some of the paintings must have dated back hundreds of years.

"This is what is known as the hall of heroes," said Dekel. "On these walls are representations of those wizards throughout history that have proven to be truly great."

Billy gazed around at the images and promptly recognized the portraits of his three instructors.

"Yes, you can see that the portraits of your teachers hang here as well," said Dekel. "They, like all the others, have the exact same thing you received when drinking from the fountain."

"But that's just it sir," said Billy. "I don't think it's fair I got to drink from it when the other students did not."

"The other students had no need to drink from it," said Dekel. "For they already had that which you received... There was no magic in the water my boy."

Dekel ran his old fingers through his long grey beard as he grinned from ear to ear. "Do you remember what was engraved into each pillar atop Cloud Shadow Tower?"

"Focus?" Billy replied.

"Correct, Mr. Huddle, and on top of those pillars of focus is where one finds the Fountain of Faith. You always had the magic in you, but until you believed in yourself, you could never have focused it from within. There was no magic in your glass, only water. However, by drinking it, you received a belief in yourself, and with that belief came your power."

"You mean the water... was just water?"

"Just water," said Dekel. "Nothing more, young wizard. Now enjoy the rest of the evening with your friends. You have surely earned it."

Chapter Ten
Have wings, can travel

As Billy arrived back at his room, he found the other students buzzing with excitement in the hallway.

"Did you hear the news?" Joey asked. "This is going to be amazing!"

"What's going to be amazing?" asked Billy.

"Tomorrow," said Shadow. "We will all be given the opportunity to ride the winged Pegasus of Mystaco Mountain."

"You mean the flying horse?" asked Billy as his eyes opened wide. "We get to ride them?"

"Not just ride them," said Joey. "We get to race them!"

The next day, the students gathered on the lawn as they had been instructed the night before. Filled with anticipation, they waited for the arrival of their instructors.

"Has anyone ever ridden a Pegasus before?" asked Lilith. "I do hope the creatures are… controllable."

"Has anyone ever even seen one before?" asked Joey. "I've only heard stories about them."

Scartail stepped in front of the other students, rudely pushing Warden aside. Of course, Warden said nothing. It was fairly common knowledge at this point that the boy didn't speak except for whispering the incantations that accompanied his spells.

"The Pegasus may be an amazing creature," said Scartail. "But the fact of the matter is that they are still creatures. They are ours to control. So if you are strong enough, the beast should obey you."

"That idea worked real well for you with the eagle, didn't it?" laughed Joey.

Scartail hissed and would have probably started a confrontation if a large wooden door had not opened at that moment, drawing everyone's attention. In walked Professor Conch dressed in his traditional robes, carrying goggles in his hands. He smiled eagerly as he approached.

"I do love this so," he said, handing a pair of goggles to each student. "There is really nothing in the world quite like it!"

"Professor Conch, are we really going to ride the Pegasus?" asked Billy.

Professor Conch laughed. "Whether you are or are not capable of riding a beast as magnificent as the Pegasus is still yet to be seen. I will tell you this though, you are indeed going to try."

From the wispy clouds above, a high-pitched neigh resounded through the temple walls. Looking up, the students saw six amazing winged horses pulling a large wooden carriage through the pale blue sky. Each steed was brilliantly white, with large feathery wings cutting through the air. Nero sat atop the carriage, guiding the animals down and landing them softly on the lawn next to the children.

"Whoa!" said Nero chuckling. "Did someone call for the take-flight taxi service?"

"Indeed we did," said Conch. "If you will be so kind as to transport our students to the top of Mystaco Mountain, I will meet you there to observe them taking off on their unforgettable flights."

With a wave of Conch's wand, the door of the carriage swung open and the students got on board. With a shaking of the reins, the winged wonders pulled the carriage back up into the sky.

The inside of the carriage was finely made with cushioned seats and red silk linings. Without windows, the cool breeze filled the cabin as it traveled gently through the air.

"First the Journeyman Ship, then teleportation by widdlebug, and now this," said Shadow. "Is there no limit to the ways we can travel?"

"I hope my young wizards are enjoying their traveling arrangements," yelled Nero back to the students. "Nothing but the absolute best for my young friends."

Nero guided the Pegasus down to a clearing at the top of a flourishing mountain, that was completely blanketed with vibrant plants and flowers. Clover filled the hillside, and a small fountain sprang up from the center of the field. The students climbed down from the carriage and stood, in awe of their surroundings.

Nero unhitched the creatures from the carriage, allowing them to drink and graze.

"Won't the beasts run away?" asked Scartail. "Should we not leave them tied?"

"They know exactly what they are here for," said Nero. "Quite brilliant creatures they are."

"Why aren't we just taking off from the temple grounds?" asked Joey. "Seems like it would have been much simpler."

"Have you ever had to clean up after one of these beasts," Nero asked, laughing. "Extremely unpleasant indeed."

Warden quietly walked up to one of the grazing animals.

"Don't dare to try to bother them while they are grazing, Mr. Fallow," said Nero. "They get a great bit grumpy when they have their meals interrupted, and a swift kick to the head from a Pegasus would be the end of you."

The Pegasus seemed quite tense as Warden reached out with both arms. It pawed at the ground as if it was disturbed, but then laid its head into his hands. Warden softly ran his fingers through its mane.

"Well I'll be," said Nero. "You have quite a way with them I see."

The largest oak tree in the grove began to creak loudly, then split apart vertically in the center of its trunk. The opening continued to widen, and Conch walked forth from the trunk of the tree. Behind him, the opening slowly closed, until no evidence remained that the tree had ever opened.

Conch dusted off and straightened his robe. Putting his fingers in his mouth, he gave a loud sharp whistle. The Pegasus stopped grazing and quickly ran to him.

"Are you all ready to see what our young wizards are made of?" said Conch, scratching behind one of the beast's ears.

"Students," he said, "it will be your responsibility to take these beautiful creatures through a series of golden rings as quickly as you can. Please wear the goggles I have provided for you, for a bug in the eye makes for a most unpleasant flight."

The students put on their goggles as Conch waved his wand towards the sky. Several golden rings appeared, floating magically and moving off into the distance. Soon, only the first ring could be seen.

"Only after you have negotiated your way through all the rings will this phase of your training be complete. Do not deviate on the journey. Stay strictly on the path from golden ring to golden ring. Now, mount your steeds and be off!"

The students climbed up onto their mounts carefully. The Pegasus were quite gentle at first, but quickly filled with energy once mounted. Billy's steed let out a thrilling neigh and bursting into the air, headed for the first ring.

"How do we fly these things?" Joey yelled with the wind racing in his hair.

"I'm just trying to hang on," replied Billy as they reached the first ring.

Shadow leaned forward and his Pegasus swiftly dove in the air. "I think all we have to do is shift our weight and they will respond to us," he said.

After flying for over an hour, the party was quite spread out. Billy and Scartail found themselves surprisingly far ahead of the others.

"You know there is no way a *wannabe* wizard like you is going to complete the rings ahead of me," said Scartail. "You haven't got it in you."

"We will just see about that," said Billy as he raced ahead.

The two boys flew through the air, battling for the front position. One of them would lead for only a short time before the other would race back ahead. The two Pegasus seemed to love the competition, bumping into one another and battling with every flap of their majestic wings.

As they flew, the sky grew increasingly dark. Black clouds pressed together and the Pegasus grew tense and worried.

"I'm headed down," Billy shouted through the wind as he guided his ride below the stormy weather. "It doesn't seem safe."

"Do what you want," said Scartail as he raced on into the darkness. "I knew you lacked the courage to be a real wizard."

Billy dropped down, flying just above the tree line. The branches were without leaves and almost seemed to reach up with the purpose of grabbing him and pulling him below.

Suddenly, two dark creatures rose just behind him from the forest below. The creatures moved closer and Billy could see they were without form, seemingly made of an eerie black smoke. As the ghostly figures moved along each side of him, he noticed that under their sooty, vapor-like hoods, their faces were menacing skulls with glowing yellow eyes.

The creature on his right reached out for him with his bony hand. Billy's Pegasus dropped down into the trees to avoid the creatures grasp, deftly swooping in and out of the growth.

Ahead, Billy saw a little straw-roofed cottage in a small clearing. An old man stood in front of it with a wand in his hand, pointed at Billy.

"*Pessimus Infitalis,*" the man said as a spiral of blue energy raced out of his wand and shot right over Billy's shoulder. Billy looked back to see the creatures that had been pursuing him flying off into the distance, carried away by the spiraling blast.

The Pegasus landed in front of the old man and walked right up to him.

"Capernicus, you old rascal," he said. "What have you got yourself into... and who is your new friend?"

"I'm Billy... Billy Huddle. Thank you for your help," he said climbing down.

"'Tis nothing at all child. What did the soul eaters want with the likes of you anyway?"

"Soul eaters...?"

"Yes. Death spirits, soul eaters... whatever you choose to call them makes no difference to me. I've lived here a long time and I haven't seen one since... well... not since things were a bit darker."

"I don't know," said Billy. "I've never even heard of them."

"Well... by all means lad, come inside," said the man. "My name is Rupert Tinsel. Let's see if we can't figure some things out."

Billy followed Rupert into his cottage, leaving his Pegasus grazing outside. The house was very quaint, with dirt floors and a large pot bubbling over the fire.

Mr. Tinsel walked over and prepared a bowl of the soupy brew and gave it to Billy.

"Do eat up now Billy," said Mr. Tinsel. "An aspiring young wizard must keep his energy up."

"You know I'm a student of the temple?" asked Billy.

"Of course I do. Why else would a young man be clothed in a robe racing a Pegasus through the forest. I know many things, lad... many, many things."

The broth was warm and comforting to Billy, and Mr. Tinsel stared at him intently as he sipped it. Mr. Tinsel's wrinkled brow reminded him a bit of his old friend Mr. Richardson, but this gentleman was far more joyful than Mr. Richardson had ever been.

Mr. Tinsel drew close to Billy, only a few inches away. "Billy... I hate to tell you this, I really do."

"Tell me what?" Billy asked, pausing from eating his soup.

Mr. Tinsel stopped staring and walked over to his sink. "People are not always what they appear to be, son."

"I've heard that before," said Billy. "An old woman with healing magic told me the same thing."

"What I fear she didn't tell you is that someone who has been very close to you is actually an exceptionally strong enemy," said Mr. Tinsel. "Not just to you, but to the whole world."

"My enemy... Who is it?" Billy asked.

"The future is still very cloudy," said Mr. Tinsel. "Much is yet to be written. It will be made clear in time, but for now keep your eyes open and your mind sharp."

Billy finished his broth and Mr. Tinsel placed his bowl into the sink.

"Well lad, I think you have kept your instructors waiting long enough. I will tell Capernicus to take you back to Mystaco Mountain with great haste. I'm sure your friends are most worried about you."

Mr. Tinsel walked Billy outside and helped him back onto the Pegasus. The steed lowered his head and burst into rapid flight just after Mr. Tinsel had whispered to him.

"And do tell Professor Dekel his good friend Rupert said hello," he called up to Billy as he flew away.

With the wind getting much colder and the sun starting to set Billy made it back to the clearing.

"Where have you been?" asked Joey as Billy landed.

"We ran into a little problem," Billy replied.

Conch held the Pegasus steady as Billy climbed down. "A problem?" he asked.

"Yes, soul eaters... two of them."

"Soul eaters...?" asked Conch. "How can you be so sure?"

"That's just what Mr. Tinsel called them," said Billy. "He helped us get rid of them and then helped me get back here."

"Students, get into the carriage at once and Nero will take you back to the temple," said Conch. "Mr. Huddle, you will be traveling with me."

The other students quickly loaded into the carriage. With a gentle shake of the reins, Nero had them gliding back toward the temple. Silently, Conch led Billy over to the large oak tree that he had emerged from before.

Reaching out and placing his wand near the trunk, it opened just as it had done before.

"After you, Mr. Huddle," Conch said motioning to the opening of the tree.

Billy walked into the opening in the tree and found himself entering what served as Dekel's office. Looking back, he saw Conch enter the room through a large wooden wardrobe behind him.

"Don't be so surprised Mr. Huddle," he heard Dekel say. "Inter-dimensional gateways are fairly common these days."

"Professor Dekel," Conch said. "This young man claims to have seen... soul eaters."

"So he has," said Dekel. "I felt the disturbance as well, though very faint it was. And this sighting was confirmed by...?"

"Mr. Tinsel," Billy quickly said. "He told me to tell you hello as well."

"Mr. Tinsel my old friend." Dekel walked over and closed the wardrobe they had entered through. "Did he tell you anything else?"

"Yes sir... He said someone who was very close to me was actually one of my enemies. That he was everyone's enemy."

Dekel cleared his throat. "And I bet that old codger left it at that didn't he... without any further explanation at all. That's just like the old hermit."

"So what are we going to do?" asked Billy.

"What you are going to do Mr. Huddle, as are all the other students, is to take an early vacation home while we make sense of this matter," said Dekel.

"Yes," said Conch. "You have all worked extremely hard since arriving and a little vacation time will do all of you some good."

"But sir, there has to be something we can do to help," said Billy.

"What you can do," said Dekel, "is enjoy your free time with friends and family. There is much training still to come."

Chapter 11

Home is where the wizard is

$\mathfrak{S}$itting in Joey's room in the temple, Billy tried to understand what he had been told again by another mysterious wizard.

"It was just like we were told by Mrs. Templeton, but this time it was made very clear that the enemy was someone close to us," Billy said.

"Who is Mrs. Templeton?" asked Shadow, standing in the middle of Joey's cluttered room. "Is she a friend of yours?"

"You could say that," said Joey. "She is a healer from my town, and a darn good one too. She told us that people weren't always what they appeared to be."

"And this Mr. Tinsel," said Billy, "who just happens to be a very good friend of Professor Dekel, said someone that is close to me was really the enemy of all of us."

Billy walked to the door, staring at it as if someone would come busting in at any moment.

"Who do you think it is?" asked Shadow.

"You know exactly who I think it is," replied Billy.

"Scartail," said Joey. "It has to be him."

Billy fiddled with the green amulet he had won during the student's challenges.

"I know that's who it is. You've seen how he's acted since he has been here…like he was different than everybody else, better than everybody else."

Joey walked over and put his arm around Billy. "I know he was none too happy when you won that intercessory amulet over him," he laughed. "Rubbed his reptile butt the wrong way, that's for sure."

"For right now though, we need to keep it quiet about him," said Shadow. "Until we can prove something I don't think it's too wise to make accusations. Instructors wouldn't like that at all."

"As much as I hate it, I agree," said Billy. "The last thing I want is to give Krishna yet another reason to put me on his bad side."

The next morning, the students were met outside their rooms by none other than Dekel himself. They gathered their things and followed him down the corridors quietly. The halls were deafeningly silent and the statues that once seemed almost alive, were eerily cold.

Walking with his arms crossed, Professor Dekel addressed the students without looking back. "I know some of you are quite curious as to why you are receiving this unexpected early vacation time, and rightfully so."

The students continued walking, with the sound of their footsteps bouncing off the stone walls.

"Needless to say," said Dekel, "it appears there is the possibility that an evil presence has surfaced. It is not your concern at this time, but you do have the right to be told."

"Is it... *the* evil presence?" asked Lilith.

"At this time we do not believe that to be the case," said Dekel. "Still, during your time away I and the other instructors shall be evaluating many things."

Professor Dekel led the students into a massive room. The walls as well as the floors were heavily padded and soft to the touch.

"Before you leave I would like to teach you one more spell," he said. "This spell was taught to me by a very dear friend and can be quite useful in a variety of situations."

Dekel waved his wand in a circle above his head and a variety of very menacing creatures appeared throughout the room. Imps, goblins, and other vicious beasts stared at the children and their professor, but did not move.

"Do not be alarmed, students," said Dekel. "These are merely illusionary representations that will be used in my teaching of the repellence of evil spell. They can do you no harm."

The students stood on edge, gazing at the array of frightening images. They may not have been real, but that didn't make them any less frightening to the students.

"When repelling the forces of evil, it is important that you focus on the absence of that evil. Your heart as well as your mind must feel the relief and comfort of knowing that it can do you no harm. Once that feeling has filled every inch of you, point your wand and say the words, *Pessimus Infitalis.*"

At that, a blue swirl poured from Dekel's wand and vaporized the goblin that was before him.

"Now students, please line up behind Mr. Huddle and demonstrate for me this repellence spell."

"Why behind that loser..." Scartail whispered under his breath.

Billy and Joey glanced at one another, overhearing Scartail's murmuring. Standing with wand in hand, Billy tried to remember what Professor Dekel had instructed him. Focusing on an imp, the thoughts of the terrorizing creatures from his travels to the Journeyman still haunted his thoughts.

"Mr. Huddle," Dekel said, "the past means absolutely nothing. Where you came from... how you got here... they both mean nothing compared to who you are."

Billy felt a warmth flow over him, like the sunrise on a hot summer morning. It's not that he didn't still have fear, but the fear didn't matter compared to his desire to send that fear away.

"*Pessimus Infitalis*," he said, sending the blue energy bursting from his wand and engulfing the image of the imp before him.

"Very good Mr. Huddle," said Dekel. "Very good indeed."

Each of the other students exhibited different degrees of mastery in performing the spell. Scartail sent forth a blast so powerful it was almost blinding to watch.

"That is how a real wizard performs the spell," he whispered to Billy as he walked to the end of the line.

Billy nudged Shadow's arm as Scartail walked past them. "Do you see what we mean?" he whispered.

"That is quite impressive, children. You have indeed come a long way in your short time here at the temple," said Dekel. "The level of growth and magical application you have shown rivals any of the classes that have graduated before you."

Dekel walked a few steps away from the students and began spinning his wand in tiny circles. Gradually, a small glowing disc formed. As the size of the circles Dekel spun with the wand increased, so did the size of the glowing disc, until it was more than large enough for a student to walk through.

"This portal will be used to take each of you back to your homes," said Dekel.

"But what if we want to stay?" asked Billy.

"Yes," added Scartail. "We can be of a greater benefit here than we can be in our homelands. I choose to stay."

The other students nodded in agreement. Over the brief time in the temple, it had become more than just a place to train, and each felt strongly tied to it, as well as to their instructors.

"Hear this," said Dekel. "It has been decided that each of you shall indeed be going home during this unsettled time. It is not a decision you shall make, for it has already been made for you."

Dekel lowered his wand and his face became especially somber.

"Before you leave, however, each of you must take the binding oath," he said. "First, your loyalty must be to that which is good and just. Will you always lay down your own personal gains and triumphs for that which is righteous for all?"

"Yes sir," the students all agreed.

"Second, will you only use what you have been taught for noble purposes, never as a means to impress, and always in the responsible manner in which we have instructed you?"

"Yes sir."

"And lastly, when we call on you to return, and we will call on you to return, will you come back to the temple immediately, trusting in the decision of your instructors ahead of your own and therefore, honoring them as well as the teachings of the temple."

"Yes, Professor Dekel."

"Students, let me not understate how extremely proud we are of your accomplishments," said Dekel. "If you would now please step through the portal... and do enjoy your time with your families."

One by one, the students disappeared into the portal. As Billy stepped through, he was surrounded by a blur of light, as if every known star was racing by him faster than his eyes could see.

Suddenly, he found himself lying on his back, staring up at a familiar face.

"Are you alright?" asked Joey. "That was awesome wasn't it? We made it back… we're just outside Turnshire."

Billy got to his feet and dusted off his robes. Almost instinctively, he reached to his side, checking to see that his wand was still in place. It hadn't been long since the last time he was in these very woods. But now, after tapping into the magic within him, these woods felt much more peaceful, much more like home.

"Awesome isn't the right word," said Billy. "That was unbelievable!"

The two boys walked towards the town and talked about the wonderful things they had experienced at the temple. They laughed about Nero's jokes, and how Billy first arrived at the temple trying to swim in two inches of freshly cut grass. They talked about the new friends they had met, and tried to figure out why it was that Warden never seemed to talk.

"Hey Billy, why do you think Scartail wanted to stay at the temple so much? Think he was up to something?"

"He could have been, but as much as he brags I don't think he has as much magical power in his whole scaly body as the instructors have in their little fingers," said Billy.

The two boys continued to talk and laugh as they made their way into town. Walking down the main street, they were frequently stopped by townsfolk wanting to say hello and ask them questions. Mr. Standish greeted the boys with Joey's favorite locust honey candy in hand.

"I bet they didn't teach you how to magically make that at the temple," he said, handing each boy a piece of the golden treat.

"No sir, they didn't," said Joey. "And even if they did, I don't think anyone could make it any better than you, with or without magic."

Both Joey and Billy began to get butterflies as they came to the front porch of the McGregors' home. After all, Mr. and Mrs. McGregor were Joey's parents, and not Billy's, but no man or woman had ever treated Billy more like a son than they had.

"Do you think they will recognize me?" asked Joey nervously as he straightened his robes.

"Are you serious," said Billy. "They are your parents; of course they will recognize you."

After a couple nervous knocks , Mrs. McGregor came to the door. She stood there staring at the two boys, and then her eyes began filling with tears.

"Joey… Billy… is it really you?" she asked grabbing both boys around the necks and hugging them tightly. "I can't believe you have come back already! Come in, come in, I know you two can use a good home-cooked meal."

"We got a little early vacation time mom," said Joey, "and yes, a home-cooked meal would be great! I tried my hand at preparing hotcakes at the temple, but they were nothing compared to what you make."

"Yes," added Billy. "I think they were a bit gritty."

The boys laughed as they sat down at the table and Mrs. McGregor began rushing around the kitchen. She was determined to make the boys a feast better than any they had ever eaten in their lives. Mr. McGregor came walking in the front door carrying the large ax.

"I'm home dear," he said.

"And you are not the only one," said Mrs. McGregor. "We have two young wizards dining with us today."

"Well would you look at that," said Mr. McGregor greeting the boys. "I would have never guessed I'd come home to two young wizards!"

"Yes sir," said Joey. "Billy didn't even know he could do magic until we got to the temple, and now he's as good as anyone!"

"You must be quite proud Billy," said Mr. McGregor. "You even have robes, a finely crafted wooden wand, and a shiny green amulet. A magic one I would bet."

"Look," said Joey, pulling out his golden wand. "We both got new ones from a thing they call the Giving Tree. We don't have 'em growing like that around here, that's for sure."

"I think I'm just lucky to be there at all, much less have a wand," Billy said.

"Don't be modest," said Joey. "He won that amulet because he mastered the magic so well. He is really good. Better than his new best friend Scartail, that's for sure." The family sat down and ate the best meal either boy had ever had. All the familiar foods Joey had grown up with seemed so comforting, like finding something lost long ago. As they ate, they talked about the amazing adventures and friends they had encountered. Cloud Shadow Tower, Mystaco Mountain, and the Library of Record and Prophecy all seemed like dreams, though they had been away from them for only a short while. After the meal, Mrs.

McGregor began bustling about and gathering up the dishes to wash.

"Do you want us to help with those, Ma?" asked Joey.

"Some things won't change," she said. "A little work never hurt anyone, and it never will. You boys go help your father with the chores outside."

The boys followed Mr. McGregor outside, finding him near the stump on which the boys had chopped logs many times before, during Joey's training. Mr. McGregor sat there, quietly leaning on the ax.

"I bet you have stayed plenty busy keeping up with everything while we were away," said Joey. "While we are here for a bit we should be able to get a lot done, especially since we both know magic now."

"And because we are both a lot better at it too," added Billy.

Mr. McGregor shook his head. "I wish chores were all that was keeping the townsfolk busy right now. These are strange days around the town of Turnshire."

"What else could there be?" asked Joey. "Are the momos acting up? They generally stick to the area near Glacier Falls."

"Momos would be a fairly simple problem to deal with," said Mr. McGregor. "Lately, a new creature has been raiding the village. It's been tearing up a few people's shops and killing livestock as well. Heck, it's not even safe to go out in the forest alone anymore."

"That's terrible," said Billy.

"Me and several of the other men from the town have been making a regular walk through the forest at night trying to drive them out and back to wherever they came from, but haven't had much luck. It seems like for every creature that we kill three more of them take their place."

"Well, it's a good thing we got this early vacation time then," said Joey. "We're going to help."

"Yes," said Billy. "What we have learned so far should be very useful. Do you know what these creatures are exactly?"

"The only person who knows anything about them is old lady Templeton," said Mr. McGregor. "She said they were a sign of evil from long ago. I think she called them imps."

"Imps?" asked Billy.

"Yes, that's what she called them," he said. "Little scaly creatures with pointed ears, only a few feet tall… nasty, primitive little monsters."

"Yeah, we know what those are," said Joey.

Joey and Billy went on to tell Mr. McGregor everything they knew about the creatures, especially about how Shadow had saved them by blinding the imps with bright light, and how for some reason the imps were quite intent on taking Billy with them.

"Well, I can assure you of this. They will not be taking our Billy anywhere as long as I'm around," said Mr. McGregor. "A party is going out again tonight. We are going to be gone for a while because we're trying to see just what these creatures are up to."

"And we will be going with you. We have learned more than a few spells that will cause these creatures a great deal of trouble," said Joey.

"Tonight at sunset," said Mr. McGregor, "the party gathers near the component shop before going out. We will show these creatures what the people from Turnshire are made of."

"And make sure they know, not to come back," said Joey.

Chapter Twelve
Imps on the run

Mr. McGregor headed off to tend to his daily responsibilities and left the boys to reacquaint themselves with the town. They had both volunteered to start helping with the chores right away, but Mr. McGregor had insisted that they enjoy at least a few hours of down time before they headed off that evening to help with tracking down the imps.

"I think we'd better be brushing up on our spells a bit before tonight, don't you?" said Joey. "I would hate for a spell to fizzle in front of the townsfolk the first time they see me since I came back from the temple."

"I agree," said Billy, pointing up the hill to Mrs. Templeton's little cottage. "But first there is someone I want to see. I think Mrs. Templeton may have a few more answers than she has been letting us know."

The two boys walked up the hill to Mrs. Templeton's home. As Billy reached up to knock, much to their surprise, the old wooden door opened.

"Ahh, the two young wizards have returned so soon. And they are much more enlightened in the ways of magic... with new wands no less," said Mrs. Templeton.

"You recognized us," said Billy. "But I thought you couldn't..."

"See... Mr. Huddle?" Mrs. Templeton welcomed the boys into her home. "A true wizard sees with much more than just his eyes. I could smell the scent of the temple on you, and the aroma of one who has been touched by the Giving Tree is unmistakable."

"That's incredible," said Joey. "You never cease to amaze me."

"And I see our new young friend has finally realized there was something special about him after all. Took him long enough, wouldn't you say?"

"You mean... you knew I was going to be able to do magic?" asked Billy.

Mrs. Templeton sat down next to the boys. "Like I've said a thousand times, the ability to do magic is in all creatures. It's only the select few that have the uncanny skill to bring it out. I had a hunch about you my boy."

"Do you know what's going on with those imp creatures?" asked Joey. "Seems like they are looking for something, but no one really knows what."

Mrs. Templeton grew very still and her face became like stone. "They are looking for an evil that hasn't been around for a very long time."

"But why are they looking here. There's not any evil in Turnshire," said Joey.

"There is evil everywhere and in almost everyone," said Mrs. Templeton. "How much and what control it has over someone is different for all... but rest assured, there is at least some measure of darkness in every creature."

"Are you telling me there is evil in me?" asked Billy. "And in Joey... and everyone?"

Mrs. Templeton took Billy's hand in hers. "Rest assured young wizard, there is indeed evil within you. Your training has doused its flame, but have no doubt it is there, as it is in all creatures. There is something very special inside of you too. A power unlike almost any I have ever witnessed before."

"How do I get rid of it?" asked Billy. "I have no desire to do anything wrong, and I don't want anything you would call evil anywhere inside me."

"Sit right here children," said Mrs. Templeton. "I think we could all use a drink."

The boys sat silently, trying to understand how evil could be within either of them, as Mrs. Templeton got up and slowly walked into her kitchen. It was quite amazing to Billy and Joey that an old blind woman could get around so well, regardless of her reputation as a healer.

Mrs. Templeton returned with a silver tray. On the tray sat three cups and two bottles of liquid. One bottle was a crystal clear beverage that had bubbles gently floating to the top, and the other was a pale brown liquid. However, the bottles containing them were identical.

Mrs. Templeton sat the tray down in front of the boys, and then passed a cup out to each.

"One of these bottles is filled with a water unlike any you have ever had before," said Mrs. Templeton. "It was collected from the dew that gathers on the wings of widdlebugs on the first day of spring. It is said to rejuvenate the mind and spirit and channel the positive energies of one's Flow. You have seen widdlebugs by now, haven't you boys?"

"Oh yes ma'am," said Billy.

"Amazing creatures for sure," added Joey.

"The other bottle holds a poison, more lethal than any you could possibly imagine. It twists your thoughts and corrupts emotion. It makes you act out of anger and desire for self-gain, destroying all rational thought and logic."

The boys looked at one another and then back at Mrs. Templeton.

"Now, my question to you is this: if you already had your cups filled and had no idea what was in them, what would you do if you were presented with these two bottles and the chance to quench your thirst? Would you drink what was already in your glasses?"

Billy and Joey sat still, quieted by the possibility that a poison so hideous was sitting just in front of them. Finally, Billy plucked up the courage to respond.

"I suppose we would have to empty our cups first to make sure that we only put the good stuff in it and none of the bad," he said.

"Exactly," said Mrs. Templeton."A wise wizard empties his cup before trying to fill it with the good of the Flow. Only after you know that you are truly emptied can you be sure that you are pure and ready to be filled."

Mrs. Templeton poured each of them a glass of the clear beverage and set the bottle back on the table.

"Now drink up boys," she said. "You both have a long night ahead of you."

"Are you sure this is the good stuff you poured for us?" asked Joey.

"Positive," said Mrs. Templeton. "The bad stuff's odor is easily detected. It smells like old apples."

The boys drank their glasses and thanked Mrs. Templeton for the refreshments and the helpful advice. As they left her home, the sun was beginning to settle and they could see below that men from the town had started to gather at the components shop.

"We'd better hurry down," said Billy. "I guess the time for practice has passed. We don't want to miss the hunt."

Hurrying down the hill, the boys arrived at a large gathering of men getting ready to set off on the expedition into the woods. The men were armed with bows and other makeshift weapons, including axes and shovels.

"Glad to see you boys made it," said Mr. McGregor. "Was beginning to think you boys were going to leave me hanging on my words."

"Your dad hasn't stopped bragging since you two got back into town," said Mr. Standish. "You've made your old man quite proud, you have."

As night fell, the townsfolk lit torches and headed off into the woods. The woods indeed felt colder, and as they journeyed deeper, anxiety began to build within the men.

"Does it feel like someone, or something is watching us?" Joey asked Billy.

"I've been thinking the same thing for quite a while now," replied Billy.

Before long, the party of seventeen men (counting the two boys) stopped, and the men began to ready their weapons. They put out the torches, and all became quiet.

"Up ahead is the clearing where we have spotted most of the little creatures," whispered Mr. McGregor. "There are usually two or three of them eating there."

The men slowly and quietly crept through the forest until they gathered at the edge of the clearing. To the men's surprise, there were not three but nine imps gathered. They were dressed in leather armor and wielding what appeared to be short swords.

"This is probably a little more than we bargained for," Mr. Standish quietly said.

"Agreed," said Mr. McGregor. "Let's make our way back to town and regroup."

No sooner had he spoken when one of the imps jumped to his feet, pointing to the party of men. It yelled wildly and the other creatures quickly grabbed their weapons and began running towards the party.

"What now?" said Mr. Standish. "Do we fight or run?"

Joey stepped out of the woods and into the clearing. He pulled his golden wand from his side and pointed it towards the group of imps running towards him.

"This is our town and our forest," he said. "Now leave us alone!"

The group of hideous little reptiles continued to run towards the party but Joey held his ground. In a steady voice he said, "*Pessimus Infitalis!*" A blue energy poured out of his wand and streamed through the creatures, knocking three of them out cold.

Billy quickly stepped forward next to his friend. "*Pessimus Infitalis,*" he said with his wand raised towards the other creatures, stopping them in fear. Two more of them fell to the ground unconscious or dead and the rest turned and ran in disarray.

"It looks like the boys have decided for us," said Mr. McGregor. "We stay and fight for what's ours!"

The men chased the imps off into the woods and pursued them for an hour. Stopping to catch their breath, the men discussed what had just happened.

"I've got to tell you boys, we got more done tonight than in the whole previous month," said Mr. Standish. "It's amazing what you two have learned in just a short time. I bet those creatures won't ever be back."

The party walked back to the clearing where they had first found the imps. While four lay dead, one creature seemed merely dazed as the men gathered around it.

"Do you want me to finish it?" Joey asked.

"No," said Mr. McGregor. "We will tie him up and take him back to town. Maybe we can get some answers as to why they are here to begin with."

With the imp bound and gagged, the group made their way back to the town. Having the two young wizards back in Turnshire seemed to fill the other men with joy and hope.

"I'll tell you this," said Mr. Standish. "This is going to make things a whole lot easier. I was beginning to think we weren't going to be able to make any ground against these creatures, but now... well, they had better just watch out, that's for sure."

"I never thought the things we learned at the temple would come in this useful so soon," said Joey. "The repellence spell really is amazing!"

The men marched along, making up songs about the victory they had just achieved as they went.

Mr. Standish had always been a bit of a clown, and as he walked he sang a merry little tune.

"Monsters and villains and bad guys, beware,

Turnshire is looking for you,

The men have come from their homes once again,

To stand for what's right and what's true.

And if you may think that evil has a chance

There's something else you'll surely find,

Our two young boys from the temple returned

And with their wands they'll light up your behinds."

The rest of the party filled with joy and laughter as Mr. Standish sang his merry tunes. Grown men picked up branches from the forest floor to reenact the magic they had seen the two young men perform. Things could not have been better for the party, as confidence and high spirits were overflowing.

But that all changed when they returned to the town, a place turned on its side.

"What happened?" Joey asked looking at his once peaceful community in shambles.

The town was a mess, with fences broken and livestock lying dead in the streets. The group entered Mr. Standish's shop to find everything inside torn off the shelves.

"It must have been a trap," said Mr. McGregor. "They waited until we were a long way off from the town then raided the village."

A young boy came running into the store. "Mr. McGregor! Your house... it's on fire!"

Mr. McGregor and the others raced back to his farmhouse to find the roof of it engulfed in flames. Ash floated in the air and was starting smaller fires on the surrounding areas. Joey raced into the house closely followed by his dad.

"Mom! Mom! Where are you?" he yelled.

He raced from room to room in search, but no one was to be found. Fiery embers and bits of wood fell all around Joey, but he kept looking back over every area, hoping he might have missed her.

"Mom! Just yell... I'll get you out," he said.

Joey's dad grabbed him from behind and started to pull him out of the burning cottage.

"She is not here, son," he said.

"But how can you be sure," he yelled, fighting to get free.

Billy grabbed hold of Joey's flailing arms and helped Mr. McGregor carry him from the house. Outside, other townsfolk were busy throwing buckets of water onto the home, trying to put out the fire. Mr. McGregor and Billy held Joey down as he continued to fight, his eyes bursting with tears.

"Your mother's not in there, Joey," said Mr. McGregor. "I think the imps must have taken her. You're not helping anyone right now by acting this way."

Joey stopped struggling and sat up. He rubbed the tears out of his eyes and wrapped his arms around his father's neck.

"Is she... de...?"

Joey couldn't bring himself to finish the question he wanted so desperately answered.

"Your mom is still alive, son," Mr. McGregor said. "I'm sure of it."

"I know she is," said Billy. "If those creatures were going to hurt somebody they would have just done it here while they had the chance."

"We have to get her back," said Joey.

Billy stood to his feet, "We will get her back. I promise you!"

The fire in the McGregor's home was quickly put out by the people of the community. The house was quite damaged, but not nearly to the extent it would have been if they had arrived even moments later.

Entering the home, they looked around to see if they could find any clues as to where Mrs. McGregor was taken, or why. Things had obviously been rummaged through, and the kitchen was a wreck. Broken dishes and torn linens littered the floor of the house. Entering the bedrooms they found much of the same, with mattresses overturned and clothes thrown everywhere.

However, in the room Billy had been staying, things were different.

Though the room was a mess, much like the others, one item stood out. As Billy entered, he found the clothes he had originally arrived in folded neatly on the bed. Looking closer, he noticed something that sent a chill straight to his bone.

The creatures had drawn a symbol on his shirt and not any old symbol, but the sign of the evil one, the one he'd touched on the mirror upstairs in Old Man Richardson's house.

Billy quickly grabbed the shirt and stuffed it under his robe just before Joey entered.

"Looks like they wrecked this room, too," Joey said.

"Yes..." said Billy quietly as he stood, dazed.

"Billy, everything is going to be okay," said Joey.

Billy turned to look at Joey. "I know it will..."

"Well, come on then," Joey said, pulling Billy out the doorway. "The adults are discussing rescue plans, and I have one of my own."

Chapter Thirteen
It takes one to know one

Billy followed Joey out of the charred remains of the McGregor home. Outside, the adults were gathering to discuss the next course of action.

"What we are going to do," said Mr. McGregor, "is charge back out in the woods and not stop looking 'til we find my wife."

"I agree," said Mr. Standish. "And any imp we find becomes a dead imp on sight."

Most of the other villagers nodded in agreement before Joey stepped forward.

"It won't work," he said. "If those creatures see us storming off through the woods, they may kill her. Charging off with weapons raised won't help anyone."

"Well, it's the best idea we have," said Mr. McGregor.

"I can do this much safer if I do it alone," said Joey.

Mr. McGregor put his hand on Joey's shoulder. "You will not be doing this alone. It's too risky. I don't care how much magical ability you have."

"But Dad...," said Joey, "it's the only way."

"I agree with your dad," said Billy. "Whatever your plan is, it's way too dangerous to do alone. That's why you and I will be doing it together."

The imp they had captured in the clearing was tied in the middle of town as a warning to the other creatures and left to await the rising of the sun. If the little monsters truly hated the light, this one would get an eyeful come morning.

Mr. Standish was to take the first watch, but when the little creature awoke he quickly realized that Mr. Standish had dozed off. Bound and gagged, tied to a post, the creature looked around in the moonlight.

A stirring came from the bushes nearby as the evil creature remained still and quiet. Two more of the hideous beings came forth from the leafy growth of the bushes. They crawled up to the restrained monster and began cutting his bindings.

"You come rescue me?" the bound and beaten imp asked.

"Yes, we comes to save you," one of the creatures responded.

After the creature was freed, the three imps quickly and quietly made their way to the edge of the woods. Free of his shackles, the imp swiftly made his way through the dense growth.

"We makes our way back to the camp now, yes?" he said.

"Yes we do," replied one of his rescuers. "You leads the way, we will follow you."

The three creatures made their way ahead through the moonlight. The woods were extremely cold as light from the stars twinkled through the dense leafless trees. The once captive imp bounded ahead of the other two, as his rescuers tried to keep up.

"I can't believe the transfiguration spell worked so well," said Joey, staring down at his scaly impish hands.

"I can't believe we are wearing clothes that came off of dead imps," said Billy, pulling at the sleeve of his leathery brown shirt.

"These things are so stupid," said Joey. "He really doesn't have any idea, does he?"

"Let's just hope that the rest of them are as stupid as he is," Billy said.

The imp stopped and turned back towards the two boys and looked at them peculiarly. He raised his clawed hand and pointed at Billy, shaking his head.

"Something be wrong," he whispered in a hissy voice.

"Wrong?" said Billy, feeling himself sweat.

"Yes…" said the creature. "You musta been using much energy to save me cause you be slower than slagga mud. Let's be a going faster."

The little creature turned and proceeded forward through the woods with the boys closely following. After quite a while, the smell of burning wood and cooking meat drifted through the air. The imp paused and took a deep breath.

"We be making it back justs in time for eats," he said, walking out into a clearing.

The area was filled with tents, campfires burning just outside them. Fresh meats were skewered and roasting over the open flames. A sinister spirit could be felt in the air.

Previously, Joey and Billy had thought that a dozen of these creatures were a large group, but looking across this campsite there had to be at least a hundred. The creatures were gleefully singing songs and socializing in high spirits.

A loud trumpeting horn sounded over the crowd. All the creatures grew silent and began to move towards a large fire in the center.

"We be gathering now, we be," said the imp to the boys. "Let's sees if the leader be happy with our works."

The boys nervously followed the imp over to the large fire. All the creatures within the camp gathered around. The very sight of so many hideous creatures was an uncomfortable feeling, to say the least.

Joey whispered to Billy, "This is unreal, there have to be hundreds of them."

"SHHH! Be quiets now. The leader, he be speaking," said another fiendish imp.

To the front of the crowded gathering, an imp much larger than the others walked and raised his clawed hands to the sky.

"Tonights," he said. "We dids a great thing in finding the one the masters be wanting us to find."

The other imps roared in excitement, waving their fists in the air.

"Whiles we did not find him, we did find something that will surely helps us find him," the chief imp said. "Todays, we founds a person that will helps us gets to him."

Out of a tent, four imps led a person out in front of the crowd of creatures. The person was bound by their hands and feet and had a burlap sack over their head. The imps pulled violently at a rope tied around the person's neck, dragging the prisoner next to their leader.

"Last night, we captured the way to the one we seek," the imp said, removing the bag over the captives head. "Today, we gots his mother!"

Standing in front of the crowd, bound and beaten, was Mrs. McGregor. She was bruised and her face was flushed with fear, but she was alive.

"Mom," Joey whispered under his breath as the imps roared in excitement.

"Not now," said Billy. "We have to be patient."

Mrs. McGregor was led off back into the tent, and the crowd of imps settled back down as the leader addressed them further.

"We knows that the magic one be here close cause he has killed many of your imp brothers," he said. "Ands we knows he be havings another too, that he be teaching how to use the magic."

The crowd of monsters grew silent.

"It be easy to know who he is when he comes. He be wearing the master's clothes, and he be usings a magic stick like the master, and he will be comings."

The chief imp pointed to two others and motioned to the tent where Mrs. McGregor was being held captive.

"Twos of us will always be watching the woman to makes sure she don't be getting away," he said. "But tonight we haves done very good... and tonights we feast."

The mob of imps roared in excitement as they made their way back around their open fires. Billy and Joey shuffled off into the crowd, trying to be as unnoticed as they could.

"Wheres do you thinks you twos be going," an imp said, grabbing them from behind. "You twos save me from bad man village, so me be feeding you... to say thanks."

The two boys followed the green being back to his tent and fire, where what appeared to be a mo-mo roasted over the open flame. The flesh of the cooking creature bubbled and popped as it heated, smelling rotten to the boys.

"Here, you eats well with me," said the imp, tearing off one of the hind legs of the mo-mo for each boy to feast on.

"Thanks," said Billy, taking a small bite of the meat. "It's good... goods."

Joey smelled the leg and made a terrible face as the imp looked on. Billy elbowed him in his ribs as he took another small bite and raised his eyebrow.

"Mmmm... goods," Joey said.

After the boys had stomached as much of the foul meat as they could, and the other creatures of the camp had eaten their fill, the imps began falling asleep one by one and the grumbled murmurings of the creatures died away. The two boys lay by the fire, whispering to one another.

"Can you believe this," said Billy.

"We have to save mom," said Joey. "I think this may be our best chance."

The two boys quietly got up and made their way to the tent where Mrs. McGregor was being held captive. Walking through the camp, hundreds of imps lay by their campfires snoring loudly.

"Here we go," said Billy as they walked into the tent.

Two scaly imps leaned against the entrance inside the tent, dozing off. As the boys entered they awoke, startled.

"What is it you be doing?" one of them asked.

"We are here to relieves you," said Billy. "We wills watch the prisoner now."

The two imps left the boys alone inside the tent with Joey's mother. She was gagged and tied firmly to a post in the middle of the tent. Her face was bruised and dried blood covered much of her arms and legs. Joey reached up and removed the gag from her mouth.

"What do you want from me," she said, as Joey quickly clasped his hand over her mouth.

"Shhhh… Mom, it's me," said Joey, staring into her eyes.

"Joey…" she whispered, her eyes filling with tears. "I thought I would never see you again."

Billy quietly interrupted, "There will be time for touching moments later. Right now we have to get out of here."

Billy pulled a small knife from his belt and made a slit in the back of the tent. "Let's quietly crawl out through here. If we can make it into the woods, we should be able to make it back to the village safely."

The three of them slowly crawled out and crept through the sleeping imps to the edge of the clearing.

"Stops," they heard an imp call from behind them. "What's are you doing?"

They turned to see one imp standing pointing towards the three of them as they tried to escape, and a camp full of imps awakening and rising to their feet. Billy stepped out in front of Joey and his mom.

"Umm, we're goings to be givings the prisoners a beatings," he said. "We didn't wants to wakes you with her screamings."

"They are not going to believe you," whispered Joey.

"How can you be so sure?"

"Just look!"

Billy turned around to see not only Mrs. McGregor but Joey standing in front of him as well. "I guess the transfiguration spell wore off, huh?" he said. "What now?"

Joey stepped out next to Billy. "I sure hope this works," he said, pulling his wand from under his cloak and raising it above his head.

"What works?" asked Billy.

"*Luminous Astrum,*" said Joey. Light as bright as the midday sun burst from his wand.

"Now let's run."

The three of them raced through the woods as fast as they could with the painful shrieking of the imps behind them.

"I didn't know that you knew how to perform Shadow's blinding light spell," said Billy.

"Neither did I," said Joey.

As the sun began to come up, the group made it back to the town of Turnshire. Mr. McGregor raced out to meet his wife.

"I'm so glad you are safe," he said, wrapping his arms around her.

"We have two amazing boys," she said.

The boys told the men of town about the incredible number of imps that occupied the camp. Mr. Standish sent a couple scouts into the woods to investigate the activities of the creature.

"Let's get you up to Mrs. Templeton," said Joey. "She will be able to fix you up.

The group took Mrs. McGregor up to the old house and was met by the old woman coming outside.

"Can you help my mom," asked Joey.

"No time... no time," said Mrs. Templeton as she walked down the hill. "They are coming."

The scout returned from the woods panting and out of breath. "There's a whole army of them," he said. "And there headed right to town."

"Men, make ready your weapons," said Mr. McGregor.

The people gathered around a small fountain in the middle of town with every weapon they could bring. The fear of the townsfolk could be felt by all as rakes, axes, and hunting tools became weapons of choice.

"How are we going to know which way they will be coming from?" asked Mr. Standish. "They could attack from any side."

Looking around the town it seemed like the imps attack could come from anywhere. The entrance to the mo-mo trail was an obvious choice but the creatures could just as likely enter by Mr. Standish's shop or even down the main street of town.

"Imps are simple-minded creatures," said Mrs. Templeton. "They will attack the area with the least resistance."

At that, she raised her wand into the air and said, "*Impenetrus Domus,*" and a protective dome radiantly enclosed the town.

"I wouldn't be able to hold this shell of protection long with them pounding through it, but if I leave them a way in, they are sure to try to take it."

Mrs. Templeton pointed her other hand towards the main road leading into the town. "They will enter through there."

The large opening in the shielding barrier was easily seen, and the battle cries of the imps could be heard drawing nearer from that direction.

"Men, focus your weapons there!" said Mr. McGregor.

The noise made by the creatures suddenly subsided.

"What are they doing?" asked Billy, his wand pointed towards the opening.

"Preparing," said Joey. "They have to be."

With a loud roar that split the silence, the imps began pouring through the opening.

"*Pessimus Infitalis*," said the two boys in unison as the repellence spell flowed from their wands. The evil monsters running through the opening were blown back and off their feet, but others quickly took their place.

The arrows from the men's bows filled the air as they showered across the creatures. Grunts and growls boomed in the air as creature climbed over creature to continue the attack.

"There are too many of them," said Mr. Standish.

"Keep fighting," said Mr. McGregor as he struck down a creature with his ax. "They will not take our town!"

The two boys continued their fury of repellence spells, and imp after imp was knocked away by the force of the spells' blasts. With each spell, it seemed the next one actually strengthened as the boys' mastery increased.

Just as the tide of the battle seemed to be turning and the number of creatures began to diminish, a large glowing portal opened next to the boys.

"Young wizards, it is time," they heard Dekel's voice say from within the portal.

"But we can't now," said Joey. "We are needed here!"

"Yes!" said Billy. "Without our help, this place will be destroyed."

"Without your help," said Dekel, "The whole world may be destroyed. Step through the portal. Did you not give your word?"

"But my mom, and my dad," said Joey. "I can't leave them!"

"Go!" yelled Mr. McGregor. "Your purpose is far greater than the town of Turnshire, boys."

"But dad, I can't!" said Joey.

"You can and you will," said Mr. McGregor. "Now!!!"

Billy jumped through the portal as Joey was caught in indecision.

"Come now young wizard, it is the time of your calling," said Dekel.

Joey ran for the portal and jumping into it, he turned to see his father locked in battle with two large imps.

"I will be back," he said, as he found himself swept away in the blur of lights.

Chapter Fourteen
Things aren't what they used to be

The boys arrived back at the temple, stepping out of the portal and into the Library of Records and Prophecy. Medea stood before them, as did their friend Shadow. Both had very puzzling looks upon their faces.

"Welcome back," Shadow said as he reached out to shake their hands.

"Welcome back?" Joey replied. "My parents…
my whole town is going under, and you say welcome
back?"

"Calm down, Mr. McGregor," said Medea.
"Your parents and the others are well taken care of.
Professor Dekel has made sure of that."

"What's happening?" asked Billy, reaching out
to shake Shadow's hand. "Why are all those creatures
attacking the town?"

"I think its best that Professor Dekel answers
your questions and fills you in," Medea said. "If you
would follow me students, I will take you to him at
once."

Medea led the three students to a tower on the
edge of the temple. The students followed their
instructor up a narrow spiral staircase. They had never
been in this area of the temple before, and it seemed
much older and ravaged by time than the rest of the
temple.

"Where is it that we are going?" Billy asked,
looking up the dim candlelit hallway of the staircase.

"You will know where we are going when we
get there, Mr. Huddle," she said. "Needless to say,
things are not the same in the temple as when you left."

Reaching the top of the tower, the students followed Medea through a heavy wooden door that creaked loudly when opened. Professor Dekel was waiting in the empty room with his arms folded.

"Young wizards, I am so glad you could make it back," said Dekel. "Thank you for honoring your vows, and therefore honoring us as your instructors."

"But sir," said Joey. "My parents... My friends..."

Dekel placed his old hand on Joey's cheek and looked into his eyes. "They are in very good hands. Our three other young wizards were sent there just as you left, to continue in your absence."

"But why have us leave?" asked Billy. "Those were our friends and our home."

"You, my young wizards, had just about used every ounce of the Flow within you," said Dekel. "You continued using your force recklessly without rationing, and when your Flow completely runs out, so can your life force."

Billy looked at Joey in a bit of disbelief. "You mean we could have died," he asked.

"Reckless use of magical gifts has brought more than one wizard to their knees," said Dekel. "And yes, some to their deaths."

Professor Dekel turned and walked over to another heavy wooden door with a small barred window. "That is not the main reason why you are here now, young wizards. Much more disturbing things have been happening. I believe you, along with your feline friend here, have a much greater purpose in store."

From the other side of the door, they heard the screams of a man begging to be let free.

"Students... students... you can't leave me in here. Honor your professor and let... me... out!!!"

"Is that Professor Krishna?" Shadow asked.

"Indeed it is," said Dekel. "Shortly after you left and we had begun discussions as to just what was troubling the balance of the world, Professor Krishna became very... disturbed."

"Disturbed?" asked Billy.

"Yes," said Dekel. "He began destroying artifacts throughout the castle, saying he was cleansing it. When the other instructors questioned his actions, he turned on them and had to be put here."

"So you locked him up in jail," Joey asked, standing on his tiptoes to try and peer into the window.

"We put him in the tower of magical suppression," Dekel said. "Here his magical ability is restrained, providing safety for others as well as himself. The other professors are working tirelessly to uncover the nature of his madness."

Dekel turned and walked towards the door through which the students had entered. "But enough of this, there is something else I must show you."

Dekel led the children down the tower and to the part of the temple containing the instructors' accommodations. The children followed Dekel into a large, very well-kept bedroom. In the room, a large brass bird cage hung, its wire door swung open.

"These are Professor Krishna's quarters," said Dekel. "None of us ever remember him having a pet of any kind, yet when we inspected his room for clues, we found this."

"So he has a pet bird?" asked Joey.

"Had a pet bird," replied Dekel. "No one has been able to locate it anywhere near the temple at this point."

Professor Medea slowly and quietly made her way to the entrance of the room. She meticulously looked around, almost as if she was searching for someone or something.

"But what if we have it all backwards," she said, slowly shuffling to the door.

"Pardon me," said Dekel, "backwards?"

"Yes," she continued. "What if Professor Krishna hasn't gone mad at all, and in fact, you are all the mad ones."

She slowly pulled out her wand and pointed it towards Dekel and the students. A look like death blazed across her face, her eyes growing dark. She continued to step backwards until she was just outside the entrance.

Behind Medea, Professor Conch quietly approached with his wand raised. He positioned his wand just a few feet from her with it pointed squarely in the middle of her back.

Professor Conch spoke forth boldly. "I think that it is best that we reassess the current situation. What is right, what is wrong... it all changes with the blowing of the wind, doesn't it?"

Medea slowly lowered her wand as she turned to see Conch standing only a few feet away. He raised his wand until it was pointing at her head.

"I believe," said Conch, "that more than one wizard has realized where their true loyalties lie."

A sinister smile came over Conch's face as he held his wand high. Professor Medea screeched in laughter and ran down the hall, leaving Conch with his wand still raised at the entrance to the room containing the students and their teacher.

"He is back, old man," said Conch. "And there is nothing anyone can do to stop it."

With that, Conch waved his wand and the door to the room slammed shut. Dekel ran to open it, but it was sealed tightly.

"It's been closed by a containment spell," said Dekel. "It will wear off in time but we won't be leaving for quite a while."

Dekel sat down into a chair and ran his hands through his long beard.

"What was that about?" asked Billy. "So now all the professors have gone mad?"

Dekel distractedly raised a finger to silence the students. He sat there stroking his beard with a heavy, frustrated wrinkle on his brow. His eyes darted back and forth, almost as if he were watching something that was playing in his mind.

"That has to be it," he said.

"Professor?" Shadow asks. "What has to be what?"

"Do you remember the story you first were told upon arriving here?" asked Dekel.

"About the dark one being destroyed?" asked Joey.

"Yes," said Dekel. "As you know, three young wizards approached the dark one in the hour before he gained an immeasurable power. Together, the three of them held him in an enchantment sphere and then cast him out of our existence to a place from whence he could never be seen or heard from again."

"Yes sir," said Billy. "We all saw the vision in the hall of prophecy. We saw him get destroyed."

"But what if, Mr. Huddle, he wasn't destroyed. At least not in his entirety," said Dekel. "Just what if he was able to place a small part of himself into each of those brave young wizards that vanquished him so many years ago?"

"Wait a second," said Joey. "Are you telling us that those three young wizards were our instructors?"

"Precisely," said Dekel. "Professor Conch even still has the scar on his arm where he was almost killed by the dark one."

Shadow got to his feet and turned to pull at the door, again with no luck. "So, are you saying that now, instead of one supreme evil being, we have three?" he asked.

Professor Dekel stood and paced about the room. "No. No, this can't be right. There is no way he would have been able to place but a fraction of himself within each of them. Once we get out of here I am sure we will be able to find a few more answers."

After the containment spell wore off, Dekel and the students left the room and assessed what had happened. There was no damage done to the temple, and all the artifacts seemed to be in order. The three professors though, were gone. The students gathered with Dekel in the library to assess just what their options were.

"So what are we supposed to do?" asked Billy.

"If the dark one does have some sort of hold on your professors, it should be easily broken. Even the dark one cannot subjugate three such powerful wizards with ease. But first, we must assess where exactly it is that they have gone to," said Dekel. "That may prove difficult."

"Not quite as difficult as you may think," said Nero as he clambered into the room. "We dwarves may not have all your mumbo jumbo magic down, but we are nonetheless a clever bunch."

"Nero, my dear friend," said Dekel, placing his arm around him. "Do you have a plan for finding our professors who have gone astray?"

"You remember the robes you had me gather for professor Krishna?" said Nero. "I sewed a tiny magical lodestone just inside the cuff of each of them. I should be able to follow it, and him, wherever they go with this."

Nero pulled from his pocket the same shiny watch he used to track the dragon on the Journeyman ship and sprung it open.

"Due south of here," Nero said. "It won't be really precise, but it will at least steer us in the right direction."

The students and Dekel headed down to the courtyard as Nero started to prepare the Journeyman

Ship according to Dekel's instructions. Gathering together, Dekel sensed the nervousness and unease of the three boys.

"I know your emotions are probably going in many different directions right now," said Dekel. "Fear, anxiety, and a bit of curiosity are all very natural things in young wizards setting out on one of their first great challenges."

The students looked at one another with a sense of purpose, but still feeling quite uneasy about the dangers that awaited them.

The Journeyman Ship burst through the clouds with Nero on its bow staring down at the gathered wizards.

"Though it is only natural to have a degree of uncertainty," said Dekel, "please know that I will be right by your side, no matter what we face."

The thought of facing their instructors was a frightening one. They had seen what Krishna alone could do to the boys and to face all three of them together seemed impossible for sure.

"Professor Dekel," said Billy. "As long as you are with us we will stand by your side."

"Yes," said Shadow. "We want to help!"

From the distant edge of the courtyard, a familiar figure walked towards the students slowly with his hands crossed in front of him. As he approached, he opened his arms to embrace Dekel.

"Mr. Tinsel my old friend," said Dekel. "Your prescence is indeed a welcomed one."

"It is good to see you," said Mr. Tinsel. "If you could professor, could I spare a moment of your time?"

Mr. Tinsel walked off with Professor Dekel to an area of the courtyard as Nero gathered the ship gently down. The cheerful little dwarf bounded off the vessel with his pocket watch still in hand.

"Is all ready to go?" he asked as he hurried alongside the students. "All signs indicate that we need to head due south, and daylight is a fading."

"I don't know for sure," Billy said. "Mr. Tinsel showed up, and he and Professor Dekel are talking about something."

"Seams really important too," said Joey.

"Students," said Dekel returning. "I am sorry to tell you this, but I will not be journeying with you on this mission. Having discussed this with Mr. Tinsel, we believe it will be in everyone's best interest if you travel alone."

"What?" said Joey. "Just us?"

"Mr. Tinsel has gathered valuable information as to the location of our lost instructors," said Dekel. "They have entered a cave many miles south of the temple, for unknown reasons."

"Hold on a second," said Billy. "Not to be disrespectful sir, but you want us to go face our instructors alone, with only the handful of spells we have learned? Just in case you forgot, Professor Krishna almost ate us alive all by himself."

"And I am sure we don't want whatever happened to Conch's first students to happen to us," said Joey.

"Let us make it clear," said Mr. Tinsel. "You are not in any way supposed to engage your instructors. Your job is simply to see what it is they are up to, and return with that information."

"Mr. Tinsel believes, and I happen to agree, that going in numbers atop the Journeyman ship would easily be detectable and may result in injury to our professors," said Dekel.

"It's not our professors I'm worried about," said Joey.

"Any great use of magic," said Tinsel, "especially the magic of the Journeyman ship, would be quickly noticed by a skilled wizard."

"And that," said Dekel, "is why you will journey to assess the situation. Your powers, though they have grown greatly in your training, should still be of a level that will be undetected."

"I'm still not so sure this is really that safe," said Billy.

"Of course it's not safe," said Joey. "You pulled us out of fighting against imps because we weren't skilled enough, and now you want us to do this? There is no way we can..."

"We will do it," said Shadow. "We will be honored to do what we can to help."

"What?" said Joey.

"Listen," said Shadow turning towards the two other boys. "All our lives we have had people who cared for us and took care of us. Our parents, our friends..."

"And our instructors," said Billy, looking at Professor Dekel.

"Right," said Shadow. "They did this not because it was easy or because they had to. They did it because they wanted to help us. They wanted us to grow into what we were meant to become. And now it is our turn to give something back."

"None of us would even be here if it wasn't for others helping us," said Billy. "Why did you and your family help me when you found me at the base of Glacier Falls?"

"Because you needed help," said Joey, seeing the truth of what Shadow had said. "We will do it. Whether there are harpies, thunderbirds, or hideous dragons with Krishna's stinky breath, we will do what we can to help."

"But how do we get there?" asked Billy. "I mean, without the use of Journeyman ship."

"I thought you would never ask," said Mr. Tinsel.

Mr. Tinsel placed his fingers in his mouth and let out a loud whistle that seemed to shake the very walls of the temple. Silence followed and, as the ringing in the students' ears stopped, they heard from above a loud neigh.

Swooping down into the courtyard were three Pegasus with feathery white wings spread. The horses landed on the grass softly, and one walked right up to Billy.

"Seems like Capernicus has not forgotten you," said Mr. Tinsel.

"Now students, let me say once again you are only to go assess the happenings inside the cave," said Dekel. "Do not be seen, and return quickly with any information you may be able to gather."

The students agreed and mounted their steeds.

"If anything," said Dekel, "*anything at all* goes wrong, fly back here as quickly as possible."

Nero handed Joey his pocket watch, and the students took flight.

Shadow turned back to address those gathered one more time.

"We will not let you down... I promise!!!"

Chapter 15

Help from an old friend

The boys exhibited a much higher degree of mastery than they had on their first flights. Their Pegasus tore through the air with grace, and the creatures seemed steadier of nerve than before, as if they recognized the gravity of their mission.

"So, what is it we are supposed to be looking for?" asked Billy.

Joey opened the watch he had been given by Nero. "As best as I can tell, we just need to head towards this little flashing dot on the watch," he said. "That has to be where Krishna is."

"We need to be on the lookout though," said Shadow. "I think it would be best if we didn't get caught by surprise."

"I agree," said Billy. "We should probably land a pretty good distance away from where it's telling us to go. If we enter by foot it should be a lot harder to spot us."

The boys landed in a place they judged to be a couple of miles away from the spot Nero's watch indicated. As the boys dismounted, the Pegasus seemed unsettled in the dim, overgrown forest.

"Keep your eyes open," said Billy. "This looks a lot like where I was attacked by the Soul Eaters."

With their wands out, they slowly made their way into the dense woods guided by the watch. The forest was thick with growth, and thorny plants pulled at the boy's robes.

They heard a grumbling sound ahead and stopped.

"Why do we be doing all the boring work," he heard a creature say.

"Me be not liking this duty at all," the other answered.

Peering through the dense forest, the boys noticed a large wooden door that appeared to be the entrance to a cave. Two imps, more caught up in their conversation than their duty, guarded the entrance.

"I'll take the one on the left, and you two deal with the one on the right," said Shadow as he began to sneak around to the side.

The moist leaves helped muffle the sound beneath the boys' feet as they crept through the dense woods. Billy could see the imps' warm breath penetrating the cold air like a fog. Shadow moved stealthily toward the imp on the left and sent a blast from his wand, knocking the creature unconscious to the ground.

As the other imp spun around, turning towards the commotion, Joey leapt forth from the woods.

"*Pessimus Infitalis*," he said, sending out his own spiraling burst of energy.

The three boys stood silent outside the wooden door with their hearts pounding in their chests.

"I guess that's that," said Billy staring down out the creatures.

"We should probably get these things out of sight," Shadow said as he pulled one of the creatures across the ground by the collar of its shirt. "Wouldn't want anyone, or anything, to see them laying here."

"Agreed," said Joey. "The last thing we would want is some of these little monsters getting the idea that we are here."

With the creatures carefully hidden away in the underbrush, the boys turned their attention to the old wooden entry way. The ashen-grey door seemed to whistle from a wind blowing from its other side.

"It looks like the entrance to an old salt mine," said Joey.

Billy carefully pulled the door open with an eerie creak. "I have a feeling salt is not the only thing we will be finding inside," he said. "I doubt the imps were guarding something to season food with."

Billy cautiously led the group into the cave, their wands in hand. The cave was damp, and torches hung on the walls lighting the pathway.

"Do you think the missing professors are going to be inside?" asked Shadow.

Joey pulled out the small pocket watch. "That seems to be what Nero's watch was telling us before we entered the cave," he said tapping on the device. "But in here it doesn't show anything."

The group of boys slowly walked down into the tunnel. The floors were slippery from moisture, and became steeper the farther they walked. Clinging to the rocks that were part of the cave walls, they descended deeper down.

Suddenly, a strong gush of wind began to blow from the entrance behind them. Turning around, the boys noticed the glowing yellow eyes of a soul eater had quietly entered the tunnel.

"What do we do now," said Joey as the spirit realized the presence of the young intruders.

"There is only one way to go now," said Shadow as he sent a repellence of evil spell back towards the entrance.

The boys raced further down the darkening tunnel as the sounds of other creatures came from the entrance.

Then, the steep passage dropped off abruptly, and though it was only a few feet the boys stumbled to the ground and began sliding down the slick surface. Whisking through the tunnel, they tried to grasp anything they could to stop their descent.

"Where is this taking us?" Billy yelled.

The boys launched out of an opening in the rock and fell several feet, splashing down into a swampy pool of water.

"It seems like we fell into something's toilet," said Joey, standing up into the thigh deep water.

"But whose toilet is it?" asked Billy.

From above, the words of a familiar voice echoed off the cave walls. "Very impressive, young wizards," said Krishna. "It appears you have indeed come a long way."

"Yes," said Medea. "It appears that he was right about you, after all."

Lights from above, slowly began to grow until they illuminated the entire massive cavern. The boys had fallen into what appeared to be a large, oval arena with stone walls surrounding them. The walls were brown and jagged, stretching far higher upward than any of the boys could climb. The floor of the arena was filled with dark murky water and giant boulders stretched up out of the polluted shallow pool, spread throughout the arena floor. Dozens of imps grunted from above the tall walls that surrounded them while

Krishna and Medea stood side by side, staring down on them with blank, cold expressions.

"What is it you want from us?" asked Billy, yelling boldly up to the professors.

"We want absolutely nothing from three frightened young wizards," answered Medea, "but we must have something from you, Mr. Huddle, and we will have it."

A rusty cracking sound came from the edge of the arena, and a massive iron gate slowly began to rise. The imps struck their swords against their shields in rhythm, creating a chorus of metal drums echoing back and forth in the huge cavern.

"What is it?" asked Joey as a thunderous roar came from behind the rising gate causing the imps to cheer with glee.

"I think we are about to find out what Conch turned into when he got rid of the other students," said Billy, grasping his wand tightly.

Emerging from the giant tunnel behind the gate was a hideous creature. It stood at least thirty feet tall as it walked upright, dragging its knuckles in the murky, stinking water like a giant ape. It was covered with scales, and had a short, crocodile-like face with long sharp teeth.

"How are we supposed to defeat that thing?" asked Joey with his voice shaking.

"Forget about defeating it," said Billy. "How can we get away from it?"

The creature opened its mouth and a stream of liquid spewed out towards the boys. As they jumped away, the acidic spray covered a large boulder, which crackled as it melted into ooze.

"Take cover," yelled Shadow, sending a blast towards the creature. His spell hit the creature squarely in the chest, causing it to turn away and allowing the group to hide behind a large boulder nearby. The imps watching the spectacle hissed in displeasure as the professors looked on.

"The only way I can see us getting out of here is through that iron gate," said Joey. "We have to make it through there!"

"But how are we supposed to get by that monster?" asked Billy. "Shadow's blast barely fazed it."

Shadow looked at his friends, holding his wand tight to his chest. "When I distract it, you two run for the gate. I'll keep it busy long enough for you to get out."

"No," said Billy. "That's way too risky. You could get killed."

"It's the only chance any of us has got. I'm much quicker than both of you," said Shadow, grinning. "Besides, everyone knows Cha'tools have nine lives."

Shadow jumped from behind the rock and yelled at the creature, quickly moving through the cloudy water and away from the rusty gate. The creature let out another thunderous roar as it burst after him.

"Go!" yelled Shadow to Joey and Billy, avoiding another spray of the creature's toxic acid. "You have to go now!"

The two boys ran splashing through the water, easily making it to the raised gate as the creature stayed focused on their cat-like friend.

"Oh no," said Joey looking back. "Shadow is stuck and he has nowhere else to run!"

Shadow was trapped between the opposite wall of the arena and the beast. The creature swung its huge fist, and Shadow went diving into the water to avoid the blow. The imps cheered, pounding on their shields with every attack of the creature.

"Where did he go?" asked Billy as his eyes searched the muddy waters for his friend.

"I don't know," said Joey, "but we're not leaving him behind."

The creature pounded the water with its fist searching for shadow as the imps roared to their feet.

"The master's champion has slain the first intruder," yelled Krishna above the noise of the crowd.

The two boys raced back into the arena to aid their friend. "*Fluxi Volaticus*," said Billy, lifting a large rock out of the water and sending it hurtling toward the back of the creature.

"*Pessimus Infitalis*," said Joey as a spiraling blast flowing from his wand propelled the boulder faster than either Billy or Joey thought possible.

The giant rock struck the beast with a crash as bits of the exploding rock flew into the crowd of imps above. The creature stumbled forward onto its knees as it groaned in pain.

"Now where is Shadow?" yelled Joey.

Halfway between the boys and the beast, Shadow stood up from the murky water and began running toward the boys. The giant monster then rose, bellowing and moving towards Shadow with massive strides.

"That thing is gaining on him," said Joey. "What now?"

"Get inside the tunnel," yelled Shadow. "Hurry, I'll be right behind you!"

Billy saw the fear in his friend's eyes as he ran from the monster. As he and Joey backed into the passageway, he could feel the very pain and hurt that he knew the monster would cause if he caught up to Shadow. As the creature opened its mouth to send out more of his acid, he could take no more.

Billy took aim with his wand and without saying a word, sent forth a continuous, dense stream of energy that slammed into the creature. Shadow quickly joined his friends and turned his attention back to the monster. The beast began to slow down under the force of Billy's blast, but with great effort continued to push forward as the three boys backed into the tunnel beyond the gate.

"Somebody has got to do something," said Billy as his wand began to shake and the creature inched its way into the opening. "I can't hold him much longer."

The creature leaned forward under the iron gate as Billy stumbled backwards, still holding his spell.

"Keep him busy just a little longer," said Joey. "I have an idea."

Joey pointed his wand at one of the beast's legs. "I hope this works," he said, sending a spell racing past the creature.

"You missed," said Shadow, turning and pointing his wand at the creature's head, preparing to cast one last desperate spell.

"Oh no I didn't," yelled Joey.

His blast ripped through the large chain next to the monster that was holding the heavy gate in place. With a loud crash it fell on top of the creature, pinning it to the ground. The monster groaned in fury struggling beneath the crushing weight of the iron. Frothing acid slowly poured out of its mouth as it breathed its final breath.

"That was absolutely brilliant," said Shadow. "Now, let's get out of here."

The three boys raced down the massive tunnel, away from the fallen beast. The sounds of imps clambering down the walls of the arena to chase after the boys could be heard as they ran.

"Where to now?" asked Billy.

"Anywhere but here," said Joey. "We have to get back, to tell Dekel what's going on."

Shadow stopped in the rocky hallway and turned back towards the gate.

"C'mon Shadow, we got to move," said Joey.

Shadow pointed his wand at the ceiling and sent out a sharp blast, causing rocks to collapse into the tunnel behind them and blocking the path of pursuit.

"That should slow them down a bit and give us a little more time," he said.

The boys continued down the tunnel, still holding their wands for anything that tried to surprise them.

"Hey Billy," said Shadow. "Where did that spell come from that you used on the creature?"

"Yeah," said Joey. "That wasn't like any spell we were ever taught at the temple."

Billy looked down at his wand.

"I'm really not sure," he said. "I just saw that you were in trouble and that power just built up inside me."

The boys slowed to a steady walk to catch their breath.

"I thought about how much I hated that creature... and hated even more the thought of what it may do to you," Billy said. "Then the blast just sort of came out."

"Like the water at the falls?" asked Joey.

"No," Billy said shaking his head. "It actually felt more like a raging fire."

As they walked along the tunnel it got smaller, and the noises of the creatures behind them disappeared. Eventually, it went no further and they were left staring at a rotting wooden ladder leading them out.

"Do we go up?" asked Shadow, pulling at one of the rungs of the ladder. "It seems like it should be sturdy enough."

"What choice do we have?" said Joey as he began to climb. "It's not like we can go back."

The ladder creaked with each step they took as they climbed upward toward a door. Joey opened the door carefully, leading them into a massive empty chamber filled with ancient rock formations.

"We have been here before," said Shadow, looking around the massive room.

"Yes, we have," said Joey as he spotted a bell-shaped opening on the opposite wall that seemed to have outside light pouring in. "And we need to leave now."

They raced across the immense chamber towards the opening, when from a raised platform they heard one of their professors once more.

"Stop," said Krishna. "You can't leave until you have completed your purpose."

"We just have to get through that opening," said Shadow. "I'm sure that's the way out."

Shadow was the first to make it and looked back to see Medea send out a spell, knocking Billy to the ground. As Joey reached the opening he turned, sending a blast of energy firing back at Medea and knocking her wand from her hand. Billy stood up and sprinted towards the opening.

"C'mon Billy," said Shadow. "It's just a little bit farther."

Just a few feet from making his way through the exit, Billy heard another voice that froze him in his place.

"Come now my boy. Sit down, stay a while, I have stories to tell you," it said.

Billy turned and searched the cavern, looking for the voice he had heard so many times in his past, the same voice that had given him a reason to go on every day. The same one that he once called *friend*.

"Billy!" Joey pleaded. "What are you doing? The opening is starting to close."

Another raging blast came from the wand of one of the professors. For Billy, everything went dark.

Chapter 16
The power of friendship

With his head throbbing, Billy awakened to find himself chained to a large stone wall. Whatever spell he was struck by had not hurt him, only knocked him unconscious. As he started to open his eyes, he overheard voices and quickly decided to keep them shut.

"So what are we supposed to do with him?" he heard Krishna say in his bland monotone voice.

"We will do… whatever he tells us to do," replied Medea. "It was the master's will to keep him alive."

Billy took a deep breath and felt a sharp pain in his ribs. Grimacing, he moved ever so slightly, causing the chains to rattle.

"It appears that our sleeping little wizard has awoken," said Medea.

Billy remained perfectly still with his eyes closed.

"It is no use trying to pretend, boy," said Krishna. "We can both sense your conscious presence."

Billy opened his eyes and looked around the chamber. Two tunnels on either side of the platform to which he was bound led into darkness. In the center, between the two professors was a stone table stained with blood. The bell-shaped opening that his friends had disappeared through was nowhere to be found.

"What is it you want from me?" Billy asked as he pulled on the shackles binding his hands. "What am I here for?"

"We want absolutely nothing from you," said Medea as she walked towards him with her hands crossed behind her back, "but the master certainly does."

"And you are here because you chose to come here," added Krishna. "It was foreseen by the master, and now it has come to pass."

"What could your master possibly want from me?" asked Billy. "I'm just a boy."

"You were never just a boy," Billy heard along with footsteps coming from a side passage. "No... you were always much, much more than that."

"Mr... Mr... Richardson?" Billy whispered.

"The very same," said the old man, walking out into the light. "Why is it that you are treating my young friend so inhospitably? Release him at once!"

"But sir..." said Krishna. "The boy... his powers have grown substantially."

"Do you question me, my servant?" said Mr. Richardson in a stern voice. "I said release him... at once!

Krishna and Medea unshackled Billy then walked up and stood next to Mr. Richardson. He couldn't believe it was really the old man from his past standing before him.

"So... it was you Mr. Richardson?" asked Billy. "All this time it was you?"

"That it was my boy, but in this world I am known by another name... Arch Mage Sindor."

Billy's face grew pale as questions raced through his mind. "So you are not the evil one?"

"Evil... good... these are both mere words to describe simple actions. The line between them is too thin to even notice," Sindor said as he clasped his hands in front of him. "Power is what this world is about, and once you give my power back to me Billy, you can rule this world with me... at my side."

"But the monsters..." said Billy. "It was you that was going to hurt my friends?"

The once pale face of the old man filled with blood and fury.

"Friends? Friends!!!" he yelled. "You don't have friends here! They were just using you to accomplish their own purposes!" Sindor clenched his fist in front of Billy's face. "To them, you were just a pawn!"

"Your friends were not using you, young wizard," Dekel rebutted Sindor, entering from the side passage. "Though it does appear you may have been used."

The old gray wizard stroked the long hairs of his beard. "For dark purposes indeed, I'm afraid."

"This doesn't concern you, old wizard," said Sindor, turning his attention away from Billy. "The power that is in the boy is mine… and I will have it back!"

Krishna and Medea both raised their wands and pointed them towards Dekel.

"I believe you remember your colleagues, do you not?" said Sindor. "It would appear that you are greatly outnumbered."

"It would indeed appear so," said Dekel, still calmly running his fingers through his long grey hair. "But your plan has a few fatal flaws."

"My plan was without error," said Sindor, pointing at the two professors whom he now controlled with the power of his mind. "When I was banished by those three meddlesome wizards years ago, I sent a part of myself back down through them using their streams of energy, their Flow. I planted a seed that awaited my return."

Krishna and Medea stood, unresponsive like statues. "And now, upon my arrival, that part of me has awakened to do my bidding."

"So, Mr. Richardson... was the evil one?" said Billy as he slowly began to back away.

"That would appear so," said Dekel as he took a few steps towards Billy with his arms extended out to his side. "But he still has one major problem with his plan. In order for him to return with his full power, he would have destroyed his now fragile body while making the journey back."

Sindor laughed as he raised his aged hand and pointed at Billy. "And that is why young Billy here... became the vessel for my power."

Dekel shook his head in disbelief. "You could have never transferred that type of power into another without them accepting it willingly. The laws of magical time and space would not allow it."

A smile formed on the face of the dark wizard. "Very true... but my young friend *did* accept it willingly."

Dekel turned to look at Billy. Frustration filled the old wizard's face as a feeling of despair filled the chamber.

Billy pulled out his wand and pointed it at his old friend. "I never agreed to let you put anything inside me," he said, filling with rage. "I would have never done that! If I would have known, I would have…"

"But you did know, my boy," interrupted Sindor with a smirk on his face. "Or have you so soon forgotten?"

"Forgotten what!" yelled Billy as his anger continued to swell.

"Remember…" the evil wizard said. "I put my heart and soul into this for you, my boy."

Billy felt the blood drain from his face. "You mean… your actual soul was in the drink you gave me?"

"And you drank every last drop! Every… last… drop. My power is in you," Sindor said. "And now I'm taking it back!"

Sindor raised his wand, pointed it at Billy, and began chanting a spell much too similar to the one the students had heard in the hall of prophecy.

With a slight flip of his wrist, Dekel sent a rock in the distance crashing against the wall. The other professors turned their attention to the noise giving Dekel an opportunity to act.

"You won't win," said Dekel as he quickly pulled his wand and sent a burst of energy towards

Sindor. Sindor using his wand to deflect Dekel's blast, sending it crashing into the stone table.

Krishna and Medea turned, casting spells of their own holding Dekel in place.

"Should we destroy him?" Krishna asked with his wand fixed on the old wizard.

"Not just yet," said Sindor. "I want him to witness this world's demise."

Suddenly, a blast of energy flew past Dekel and struck Medea to the ground. Professor Conch came running from the tunnel with his wand at the ready.

"Brilliant timing as always," said Dekel as the distraction caused Krishna to release the spell holding him.

Dekel quickly gathered himself and turning his wand on Krishna, sent out a formidable magical blast, knocking him unconscious to the ground. Sindor stopped his incantation as he looked upon his two servants asleep on the ground.

"Give it up, dark wizard," said Dekel, turning his wand towards Sindor. "It would appear the tables have turned."

Sindor sneered. "You stupid old man. Do you think I would rely solely on those incompetent fools to do my bidding?"

Sindor lifted his wand and a wall of crimson flames roared up from the ground, blocking Dekel and Conch from coming to Billy's aid. Dekel took aim with his wand and sent forth an energy blast, but it was quickly absorbed by the pulsing flames.

"Leave the boy alone," said Conch, sending his own magical spell flashing into the wall of fire with no result.

"Now, where were we young Billy?" asked Sindor as he continued his evil chant.

Billy stood there, paralyzed in fear. How could someone he trusted for so long, someone he considered a friend, have simply been using him?

"Billy," yelled Dekel over the sound of the roaring flames and Sindor's incantation. "There truly is power within you, there has always been!"

"But it's not my power," said Billy. "It has been someone else's all along. I can't control it."

"Have faith, young wizard," yelled Conch. "Remember your friends, and who it is you are fighting for!"

Sindor pointed his wand at Billy's chest, and gradually a swirling black energy emerged. It moved strangely as the light from the wall of flames bent toward it, pulled in by its incredible power.

"At last," said Sindor. The power will be mine...! Again!!!"

The black energy raced out of Sindor's wand, as time itself appeared to stand still. The dark blast struck Billy in the chest, and instantly he began to feel his breath being taken away, his heartbeat slowing.

Gazing into Sindor's face, the aging process was reversed. Sindor's wrinkles vanished, as the old man appeared to be regaining his youth.

"Yes!!!" Sindor yelled with the power of youth in his voice. "I am being made whole once more! Nothing shall stand in my way!"

"What are we to do now?" asked Conch as he sent another useless blast into the wall of flame. "He's going to be killed!"

Dekel lowered his wand and walked slowly up to Conch. "There is nothing that I or anyone can do now," he said. The fate of that boy... of this whole world... rests solely with him now."

With the black energy pulling from the center of his very soul, Billy saw all that he ever was flashing before his eyes. He saw himself sitting in Mr. Richardson's kitchen as he hung on every word of his stories, being swept away to a magical place. He felt the warmth of the McGregor family meals, and their generosity and acceptance in always treating them like their own son.

"The world will be laid to waste at my feet and tremble at my very breath," said Sindor as the wall of flames rose with his power.

Billy seemed completely lost as he closed his eyes and drifted into a state of living death. Memories continued to flash through his mind like the rapidly turning pages of a picture book. Shadow's bravery and courage... Joey's humor and compassion... Professor Dekel's steady hand on his shoulder as he told him it would be okay.

Sindor screamed in a soul-shattering voice, "my resurrection as the dark ruler is nearly complete," as one haunting image froze in Billy's mind...

Darkness...

A vibrant world filled with life was empty and barren. The noble temple lay in ruins and the professors Billy had grown to respect and admire were broken shells of themselves. His friends were but captured prisoners, beaten and bloodied for the amusement of one hideous man as darkness ruled the planet.

"This can't happen," Billy whispered as he felt the heart in his chest begin to beat with a sound like thunder. "I won't let this happen..."

"Noooooooo!!!" Billy pointed his wand into the black energy coming forth from the dark wizard and sent out his own radiant blue blast.

"It's too late," said Sindor as the opposing energies met between them in a violent crash. "I have already regained far too much power for you to do anything to stop me!"

"I can't let you destroy this world," said Billy, as the dark energy began to win the struggle between them. "I won't let you!"

"You have no say in this matter, you foolish child," Sindor said as he grasped his wand with both hands and increased the power of his spell. "I hold all of the power now!"

The evil energy was only inches away from Billy's wand and all hope that remained seemed held in a tiny blue pulse extending outward. Only that small amount of energy stood between everything he was fighting for and the destruction of the world.

"Billy," said Dekel. "Use the power from within. Use it now!!!"

The amulet of intercession Billy proudly wore around his neck floated upward before him, pulled toward Billy's extended wand.

"I...... will not... let you hurt my friends...!!!"

Billy screamed as the gem held in the amulet shattered into a million pieces. The once-blue stream of energy from his wand suddenly turned green and began to grow.

"What are you doing?" yelled Sindor, as his dark spell ceased. "This cannot be happening!"

The large mist of green energy from Billy's wand swirled and spun until it finally took form. A ghostly creature stood between young Billy Huddle and the dark wizard.

"It's... it's a wyvern," said Billy as he fell to the ground in exhaustion.

The creature let out a roar that seemed to shatter the heavens themselves as Sindor stumbled backwards, then turned and with the light-footed steps of a spirit walked towards Billy, its tongue tasting the air.

"You... you have green eyes..." whispered Billy as tears began to fall.

The creature turned and with a giant leap and a downward sweep of its wings, grabbed Sindor in its jaws. With Sindor as its captive, it flew straight through the roof of the cavern and disappeared.

The wall of flames that had been isolating Billy from his instructors vanished as Billy sat holding his shattered amulet in one hand and his wand in the other. Professor Dekel and Conch ran to Billy as he tried to speak.

"Joey... Shadow...," said Billy. "Are they..."

"Rest young wizard, for your friends are safe," said Dekel. "You made sure of that today."

Professor Conch held Billy's head and carefully laid him down as tears continued to pour from his eyes. "You, my young wizard, have excelled far beyond any could have imagined," he said. "Truly amazing indeed."

"But what about Mr. Richar... The dark wizard?" asked Billy. "Is he dead?"

"Not dead," said Dekel laying his hand on Billy's chest, "but his power has definitely been suppressed, and should be for quite some time."

Dekel pulled on his beard as he paused in thought. "For now, he is in isolation, but there will come the day when he shall try to regain his power once more."

Conch put his hand on Billy's head and looked into Billy's tear-filled eyes. "And when that day comes... and that day will come," he said, "with your help and that of your friends... we will be ready."

Made in the USA
Charleston, SC
06 October 2011